Alan

SHORT STORIES
FROM
LOCKDOWN

ALAN MACKENZIE AND
RICHARD CLIFTON

CONTENTS

TERRA INCOGNITA
Alan Mackenzie

It had taken hundreds of years to perfect the ion-drive for spaceships to reach half the speed of light. A few more centuries were needed to build the mother ships to send out beyond their solar system in the search for habitable planets. They had spent decades mining titanium, vanadium, and tungsten to develop the hardest hulls to withstand space debris and long-term radiation and had perfected cryogenic systems to preserve life for the longest space journeys. Robot probes had first been sent to promising star systems to see where life might be possible, and they had waited years for the results to return. Many had then died in the first subsequent manned explorations beyond their planet. But despite the wars, revolutions, climate change, pollution, population growth and, indeed, all the ills that so-called civilisation is heir to, they were finally on their way to exploring the farther reaches of the galaxy. Ten mother ships had been launched each with five manned spaceships with a mission to find a planet to colonise.

At some six billion kilometres from their objective Commander Bok of space mission Five was woken by the on-board computer from his cryogenic sleep. He and his crew of three had spent five years in a suspended animation as his spaceship travelled through the cosmos at some 300 million miles an hour. They were now entering a planetary system and approaching a medium sized planet about 150 million kilometres from an average star. As the ion-drive reversed the thrust their speed reduced and they had a further week before they were in sight of the planet.

The preliminary probes had shown the planet to be much larger than their own with a viable but dense atmosphere of nitrogen and oxygen. Gravitational pull might be a problem but there appeared to be significant quantities of water. Commander Bok was optimistic that colonisation would be possible.

After five days travelling through this strange solar system with numerous other planets, including two large gas giants, they finally saw their objective. The planet was, indeed, some five times larger than their own and 70% of its surface appeared covered in water over which they could see clouds circulating. A moon orbited the planet at a distance of around 400,000 km. The spaceship moved closer and settled into an orbit at around 100,000 km in order to make final preparations for landing.

"This might just be the one." Commander Bok smiled to his colleagues Denek and Arak as they contemplated the blue sphere.

"Atmospheric composition appears reasonable. No signs of significant volcanic activity. Abundant water and significant landmass. Electromagnetic radiation levels appear to be normal." Denek was the scientific officer charged with preparing the spaceship for landing. "My only concern is that gravity will be significantly higher than at home. The planetary mass is at least 5 times higher. No evidence of life forms as yet but these would be difficult to discern at this distance."

"Send a preliminary report anyway and prepare to land. I suggest we aim for that large land mass in the southern hemisphere." Bok knew that the report would not get to their mother ship for several years, but it was important for the leadership to know they had arrived.

The spaceship moved to a lower orbit and deployed its heat shields to meet the atmospheric resistance. Bok and his colleagues strapped themselves in and prepared themselves for rapid deceleration. He had practised such landings before on his home planet, but they were always fraught with danger. He knew that you could plan for everything except the unexpected and this was more than likely on an unknown planet. In the event the descent was smoother and slower than he had anticipated despite the high gravitational pull. There were no violent storms and they could watch as a vast area of blue water gave way to a flat plain which lay between two mountain ranges. The reverse thrust worked perfectly and as the engines cut out the spaceship landed with a sigh on a perfectly level expanse of what appeared to be sand.

It took several hours to complete the landing checks – heat shields, ion-drive, thrusters, coolants, internal atmosphere et cetera – but eventually Bok was able to survey through the external cameras exactly where they were. On all sides he could see a sandy plain extend to the horizon at which white capped mountains rose into a perfectly blue sky. There were no clouds and no perceptible wind. The sun was high in the sky and his instruments indicated an outside temperature of around 40°C. Above all there was no sound of any kind. All the instruments seemed to indicate that this was an area totally devoid of any life whatsoever.

"Well, Denek" said Bok "You appear to have taken us to the most boring area of the planet you can imagine!"

Denek laughed, "At least we're all still alive, boss!" Just then Bok saw a dust cloud appear on the horizon which was moving rapidly towards them travelling on rather an erratic course. Gradually they made out within the swirling dust cloud an enormous square engine moving on four wheels and belching out thick clouds of black smoke. As it approached, they could see two huge creatures sitting on top of the engine and appearing to be guiding its course. The engine was only 200 m away from their spaceship when it suddenly shuddered to a halt with an explosion of black smoke from its rear.

Bok watched the camera screen transfixed as the two creatures clambered down unsteadily from their perch on the engine and fell heavily onto the sand. They each appeared to have a head, two arms and two legs but the whole body was wrapped in dust caked rags. But it was above all the size of the creatures which was terrifying to the crew of the spaceship. They were at least one hundred times larger than their spaceship and, as they began crawling sloth like through the sand towards them one arm in turn pulling the giant body with what must have been immense effort, Bok realised in panic that they could easily crush the spaceship.

It was at that moment that Denek shouted "Boss, we have a problem. I just recalibrated the radiation sensors and all our readings up to now were wrong. The radiation levels out there are at least fifty times higher than we thought. The radiation shields will protect us for a time but not for long. We have to get out."

Bok now knew that this planet was no paradise and that the giant creatures grinding laboriously towards them were evidently dying of radiation sickness. He had no way of determining whether this was from natural causes or as a result of some nuclear war, but it was clear they had to go and quickly. He gave instructions to Arak and he heard the sound of the ion drive preparing to launch. The creatures were now only fifty metres away and he could hear their gasps and gargling. The spaceship shuddered as the ion drive thrust the vessel into the air fighting and eventually winning the battle with the gravitational pull.

On the sandy plain of the medium size planet one hundred and fifty million kilometres from a very average star, one creature had seen the spaceship take off. It turned to the other and mumbled through his blood-soaked rags "Did you see that?". The other creature coughed up some blood and stopped moving. They had spent six months in a bunker in the mountains waiting for the radiation to subside. Eventually their food and water had run out and they had had no option but to try to escape and find life somewhere on the planet. The first creature also stopped moving. The effort was too much, and it knew it was about to die. It whispered quietly to itself "I could have sworn that was a dragonfly."

Freed from the gravitational pull of the planet Bok and his crew set a course for the mothership. He accepted philosophically that this was yet another failed attempt to find a planet to colonise. But they would continue to search as would generations to come. The crew settled themselves into their cryopods and prepared for the long sleep back. As Bok fitted his six legs into the pod and cleaned his antennae, he wondered briefly how those creatures had ever managed to survive with only two legs.

THE ANNIVERSARY
Richard Clifton

I am awakened by the stinging needles of many tiny medical robots, swarming over my body. I am told the ship is already in orbit around Proxima Centauri III. The words register but as yet my befuddled brain has no clue what they really mean.

Coming to my senses after a twenty-year sleep could be compared to barely surviving the worst hangover ever. The drugs ensure I am awake and alert but, for a while, I do not remember who I am. This is disconcerting. I am forcibly reminded of the primary directive for such awakenings, but only because the words have been temporarily imprinted on my visual cortex. As the words "Don't Panic – Everything's Fine" fade from my sight and the last of the suspension fluid drains from my veins, my personality and memories begin to return, along with the reason I am here.

It appears I am Oswald Mitford, the Captain of Survey Ship "Unity", part of a fleet of vessels undertaking mankind's first tentative exploration beyond the solar system. Apparently, I have arrived.

The domed ceiling above my damp cot becomes a screen filled with flashing images and other information. I struggle to focus.

"Captain, we've struck gold here," says Unity. The ship's computer shares her name with the ship itself. She is the ship. Her usually tranquil voice betrays some excitement. "There's not only water here, there's life! The place is teeming with it."

"We were only given a 10% probability," I hear myself croak. "I thought we'd just survey and move on."

"I don't think we'll be going anywhere for a while," Unity says confidently. "We're years ahead of the other ships and we can be the first to report back." As I struggle to answer she adds: "But of course that's your decision. Captain."

"What sort of life are you talking about?" I ask.

"The things at the top of the food chain are intelligent, relatively speaking," Unity explains as more images appear above. "The biology is almost mammalian, but the body plan is more like an arthropod."

Unity waits for me to take in the images of the Centaurans. At first, I cannot tell the front end from the back end. There appear to be six limbs, which seem to bend the wrong way in all the wrong places.

All the imaginings of six hundred years of science fiction have not prepared me for the reality of the first actual alien beings to be seen by human eyes. To some, my first reaction might seem unworthy. Someone with an innate fear of spiders might be more understanding.

"Yuck!" I find myself exclaiming. "At least we won't have a problem with the crew fraternising with the natives."

Unity ignores the remark. "I've got over a hundred mini-drones active on the surface so we're starting to get a pretty good picture of what makes them tick."

"Do they know we're here?" I enquire.

"Not a chance," says Unity. "The drones are disguised as insect life and the natives are still in the steam age anyway. They have flying machines as well as locomotives though. Wood-burning airships to be precise. It's really rather quaint down there."

"Could they detect our comms?"

"They have a few primitive radios mainly on the southern continent, where things are a bit more technologically advanced, but our bands are way above where they operate."

I start to recollect the manual of first contact drummed into me during training, including Question Number One: "Is your assessment that there is no military threat?" I ask.

"Absolutely," says Unity. "But there are some golden opportunities." "Like what?"

Unity pauses for effect; "The planet has huge deposits of irridium," she says proudly. "Quite close to the surface, too."

The news sinks in. Earth had been all but depleted of the precious element when the engines of this ship and her sisters had been constructed. "We could build the next wave of survey ships here," I suggest to Unity. "This could be the hub of a second expansion."

"With a little help from the natives," says Unity, with no obvious humour.

After a pause for thought, I decide it is time for a captain to start issuing orders.

"You'd better wake up Gunther next," my voice is tremulous, somewhat detracting from my authority. It is because robot hands are massaging my arms and legs, preparing me for movement. I judge that the papal legate had better be present for the broadcast of the First Contact message to Earth and the other ships. Pompous prick or not.

By the time Monsignor Gunther enters I have exercised a little and donned my navy uniform, unworn for twenty years but still pristine. There are no moths and very little dust on board the SS Unity. However, Gunther has gone one better.

"How'd you like the new outfit?" he asks. "I just had time to download it from the Earth data stream before coming up. So, it's only about four years old if I've got my physics right. I got promoted too, by the look of it."

I look Gunther up and down, struggling to conceal my contempt. I note that the trend towards militaristic style in clerical garb has continued apace during SS Unity's long journey. Gunther is even sporting epaulettes. To my horror, ribbons indicating the honorary rank of brigadier general dangle from his weighty crucifix. That is one better than me. How ridiculous, I think, for priests to have honorary ranks.

I pause for a moment to consider what damning with faint praise could sound like, without being obviously insulting.

"Very nice, Monsignor but let's get down to business. I assume you've been briefed by Unity, as I have. What we've found warrants a First Contact message which we need to draft jointly. What we say may change the flight plans of other ships. In particular we need the follow-up ship to begin slowing down for landfall here. We'll need plenty of help to...exploit the situation here."

"I guessed as much," says Gunther. "I heard about the irridium. We should give thanks to God."

"We'll do that later," I say impatiently. "The longer we leave things, the more slowing down the follow-up ship will have to do."

I suspect that Gunther's understanding of orbital mechanics is sketchy but he surely grasps the need for urgency, doesn't he? And hour wasted now might lead to an extra week of orbital manoeuvres later. I had always questioned the need for clerics on board survey ships, but I never doubted the need for the near union of church and state which had unified the Earth, although not without a century of struggle.

"Did you get a look at the natives, Monsignor?" I ask. "Not exactly made in the image of God, are they?"

Gunther laughs. "It's their souls that count Captain," he says. "If they have any, that is. I'll need to work on some tests to determine if they are so blessed."

That will keep you out of my way, hopefully, I think to myself.

".. and if they don't," Gunther carries on. "They may still make very good workers."

I have another motive for getting the message away promptly. I want it to arrive back on Earth on a very special date, four years hence on February 1, 2183 AD. The news will ensure my place in history and probably my fortune.

After an hour or so, and a few squabbles, Gunther and I have a finished text for the message. I have persuaded him against a 2D or 3D video version by lying about a lack of bandwidth, because I think his ridiculous uniform will lower the tone. He gives the message a final scan.

"Shouldn't we mention the follow-up ship by name?" he suggests.
"It's changed recently hasn't it? They might not know."

I concede it is a good suggestion. "Yes," I say. "It was to be the SS King Edward VIII, but now it's the SS Heinrich Himmler. They started later but their engines are better."

Gunther glows with satisfaction. The next ship will be crewed mainly by his countrymen, many of whom will outrank me by many grades.

I am happy that the message will arrive on time, on the 250th anniversary of the day that the first leader declared the beginning of the empire that would endure for a thousand years.

THE GAME
Alan Mackenzie

Elsie Matthews had had enough. Her husband, John, had suddenly left her three years ago and she had been forced to get a job in a local newsagent in order to provide for both herself and her only son. Six days a week she would get up at 6 o'clock in the morning, prepare a cup of tea for her son, take a quick breakfast in the company of BBC Radio Four, lock the back door and, having closed the front door of their rented two bedroomed terrace in Alamein Avenue, walk the 10 minutes it took to the shop four streets away to open up promptly at seven. Every day at seven in the evening she would make the return journey pausing sometimes to visit the local Tesco's.

It was not that she disliked the job. The owner, Mr Khan, was pleasant and polite and she enjoyed the daily routine of selling sweets, tobacco and newspapers and gossiping to the regulars. She liked people and there was an inexhaustible supply of subjects for conversation – once you had moaned about the weather, the government and taxes, there was always the latest shenanigans of Mrs Ellis in Khartoum Place round the corner or Mr Fraser's shady deals in the market every Friday. It was a small town but there was always something going on. No, she enjoyed the rich warp and woof of the local town's busyness. But, at 50, she was tired and depressed at the prospect of her life never changing. Above all, she was worried about her son.

Robin Matthews had been a bright boy at school. Quiet and studious he had passed all his exams and managed to get into university and graduate with a mediocre degree in media studies. His mother was pleased that her son was good looking, affable and unostentatiously charming. She had had high hopes that he would get into the television or film business, that he would travel the world producing exciting documentaries or even be lured to Hollywood to work on one of those blockbuster films she read about during the quiet times in Mr Khan's shop. In short Robin had been the repository of all the hopes for a future she herself did not and would never have.

All had changed, however, after he left university. She did not, of course, expect him to get a job immediately. She knew that the economic conditions were not good, and competition was fierce. She recognised that he needed time to recuperate from the pressure of exams and the intellectual hothouse of university life. She made him meals and did his washing. In the first few weeks after he left university, they would have evening meals together during which she would gently enquire what he was doing. Robin always had an easy answer – he was working on scenarios, outlines, projects and had sent off multiple job applications and was hopeful that something would come up soon. Gradually, however, their evening meals together became less frequent, their conversations brief and sporadic and he spent more time alone in his bedroom with a computer he had bought after a summer job. As the weeks turned to months and finally to years, he became a virtual hermit in his bedroom. He seemed to have no friends, no ambition, and no prospects. In the beginning Elsie would proudly tell Mr Khan that her son was busy developing a play or film script and that he needed space and time for his creative energies. After a year, however, this explanation began to seem lame and defensive and Mr Khan no longer asked how her son was. She knew that something must be done but was not clear what. She did not know that Robin had a secret.

Robin's secret was that in the confines of his bedroom hunched over the computer he had disappeared. In the two years since graduating he had immersed himself in the Game. Here he was no longer some insignificant cipher in a boring English town but a major player in a game which reached out to countless others in all countries of the world. He was in turn Attila the Hun, Genghis Khan, Suleiman the Magnificent, Ivan the Terrible, Akbar the Great. He commanded vast armies which conquered his enemies from the Mongolian plain to Asia Minor, from Mexico to Argentina, from Japan to India. He made astounding advances in science and technology and built wondrous cities. His intellect was vast and his power untrammelled. People made obeisance to him and kissed the ring of power. He was truly a colossus who bestrode the world. And he had friends. Of course, he had friends. They were similarly ensconced in their bedrooms in Tokyo, Manila, Quito and New York and dreaming of their powers in the Game and vying with each other to dominate their imagined universe which the Internet had spawn – insubstantial but oh so real. They were all part of a communal addiction more powerful than any drug.

It was one Thursday evening two and a half years after Robin's graduation as Elsie trudged home from work through the rain that she finally decided to act. In the kitchen she put the groceries away, set the table for dinner and began to prepare Welsh rarebit. She knew it used to be one of Robin's favourites. She opened a bottle of cheap white wine and poured herself a glass. She would have to be fortified. She took her mobile phone and rang her friend June to see how she was. She had just come back from hospital after hip replacement and was apparently well. Then she went upstairs and knocked quietly on Robin's door.

"Robin, love, I'm preparing Welsh rarebit. Would you like to come down will have a nice dinner together?" She could hear no sound but the tapping of the computer keyboard.

"Come on Robin. It will be ready in five minutes." She heard a shuffling and the bedroom door inched open.

"Mum, can't you see I'm busy. I'm in the middle of something really important. Can't it wait?" The voice was vexed, impatient and exasperated.

"No, it can't. I'm just going to the bathroom. You go down and I'll be with you in a minute." She heard Robin sighing as he closed the door. She went to the bathroom, pushed the door to and listened to Robin's footsteps on the stairs. Once she was certain he had gone down to the kitchen she went to Robin's bedroom and opened the door gingerly. There in the middle of the room sat his desk, chair, and the computer. Everything around was in the dark, but the computer screen lit up the room with an image of the world. It was like the eye of some malevolent creature summoned from the underworld. She was not familiar with computers, but she knew there had to be an on/off switch somewhere. She pressed various buttons on the keyboard and finally found the switch on the desktop. The computer died almost reluctantly as the hard disk exhaled its last breath. She closed Robin's door quietly and came downstairs.

"Well, what have you been doing today?" She thought she would start with a friendly opening gambit.

"I've been busy, mum, and I've still got lots to do. Are we eating straightaway?" Robin really did not have time for this

"I thought we'd have your favourite meal and have a nice chat." She smiled and put the saucepan on the cooker. "Would you like a glass of wine?"

"No, not really." He paused, an irritated frown on his face. "Look, mum, I'll just go back upstairs for a moment and you call me when the meal is ready."

"Surely you can spare five minutes for a chat?" But Robin had already left the kitchen and was going up the stairs. Elsie turned back to the cooker. A moment later she heard an awful strangled scream and the sound of Robin's footsteps pounding down the stairs.

"What have you done?" Robin's face was red in a paroxysm of anger as he stood in the doorway to the kitchen. "Do you realise what you've done?".

"I just thought we should have a nice little chat about your future. You know we can't continue this way." Elsie was calm and measured but taken aback by her son's anger and his clenching fists. She stepped back to the sink.

"You switched off the computer." Robin's voice was incredulous. "You destroyed it. You've destroyed years of work. You've destroyed the Game." He stared at her unable to believe what she had done.

"Now, don't be silly, Robin. I just switched it off, so we'd have time for our chat and no distractions. I'm sure nothing is lost." Her voice began to tremble as Robin moved towards her.

"You stupid, fucking bitch! How can you be so stupid?"

"Robin, that's no way to speak your mother!" She began to be afraid as her son spluttered with anger. "Why don't we just sit down and discuss things?"

Suddenly Robin appeared to calm down but continued to stare intently at his mother. She had destroyed his world, but he was no longer Robin Matthews. He was Akbar the Great. As his mother's eyes grew wide with horror, he took the bread knife from the table and plunged it into her. Once, twice, three times. Elsie gasped for breath as her mouth filled with blood and she slowly collapsed on the kitchen floor. Robin stood over her, the knife still in hand, content that he had done the right thing. After a moment he heard a voice from the mobile phone on the table. Elsie had mistakenly left it on.

"Are you all right, Elsie?" It was June. "I heard these terrible noises. We must both have left our phones on. Speak to me!"

Robin picked up the phone with his left hand as the blood dripped from the bread knife in his right. He whispered hoarsely "Go away!" and switched the phone off.

It took the police only five minutes from June's emergency phone call to arrive at Alamein Avenue. The patrol car parked in front of the house with its blue light flashing and two constables went up to the front door. There was no answer to their repeated knocking and one of them then went around the back to the kitchen door. Through the window he could see Robin still standing there holding the knife and what appeared to be a body lying on the kitchen floor. He immediately phoned through to call for an ambulance and to ask for backup. He then returned to his colleague in the front to force open the front door. From the hall they could see Robin in the kitchen still motionless in front of the lifeless body of his mother. As the sirens of the ambulance and the backup car grew louder the two constables moved slowly towards the kitchen.

"What's going on here? Put the knife down, son!" They got out their tasers as Robin still did not move. "Move away from the body and put the knife down!" They could hear the ambulance arrive and the paramedics come into the hallway. They repeated "Put the knife down and move away from the body!" Slowly Robin put the knife down on the kitchen table and stood back from the body. One policeman grabbed and cuffed him and sat him on one of the kitchen chairs while his colleague spoke on the phone to CID. The paramedics confirmed quickly that Elsie was dead.

"Do you want to tell us what happened?" The policeman looked carefully at Robin and spoke very quietly. Robin's vacant stare was disquieting. "Did you kill her?"

"You don't understand. You will never understand." Robin's voice expressed all his pent-up sadness and bitterness. "She destroyed it. She destroyed my world. She stopped the Game. You cannot do that. You are not real. Only the Game is real. Only the Game is real."

JAZZ ON A WINTER'S NIGHT
Richard Clifton

At the end of a long, chilly bike ride is the promise of a rare treat: a pub offering jazz from a band with a growing reputation.

There are bike racks around the back but only a fool would leave an item of any value there. That is where the guys in the nondescript white van could work undisturbed in the darkness for half an hour. What is more, with bolt-cutters and a battery-powered angle-grinder they would only need five minutes. Forget it. I chain the bike to a tree in the front garden in the full glare of the pub floodlights. In the past I have often left my precious steed attached to the railing of a traffic island in the middle of a busy road. That is just about the safest place there is, if you can find anywhere like that. The central reservation of a motorway would be better, but there is an increased risk of death.

I am a bit late, but I cannot hear any music from within, so I guess the band have not started yet. The jazz aficionados have gathered at one end of the long bar where a drum kit it set up. Not a bad turn-out. There are even some young people.

There is a seat free at a table at the front, so I get a beer and claim it. The drummer and the bass player are standing nearby, looking a bit nervous.

Drums is also the regular MC and he soon makes an announcement that the rest of tonight's band, Trumpet and Keyboards, have been delayed by a blow-out on the M1. They will not be long, he promises.

I guess this is how it works. The locals offer to provide a rhythm section so that the main players do not have to bring too much stuff. They can just about get the keyboard and other instruments in the back of a car, but a drum kit would need a van. When you are playing for free drinks and the contents of a hat, costs need to be kept to a minimum. I wonder if they told their regular drummer they had a gig.

To my surprise Trumpet and Keyboards show up just a few minutes later, carrying the keyboard case between them. A large duffle bag, presumably containing the rest of their kit is balanced on top.

Drums says hello and introduces them to Bass. Oh, I get it. They have never met before and they are proposing to entertain us with an evening of largely improvised music. I know from experience that could be awful or wonderful, so I am not too worried.

They are soon getting unpacked. Bass is slightly built and has his usual tussle getting his monstrous instrument from its bag, Keyboards forgets he has left his organ switched on and almost blows the speakers in the pub PA when he plugs in. Trumpet finds some spit left in his instrument from last night and decides to enrich the polished floor with it. Then he leafs through some very tatty sheet music, looking for an opening number.

To everyone else's alarm Drums decides to get things moving and introduces the musicians, except himself. We all know him anyway. Trumpet makes a quick selection and hands out crumpled half-pages of musical manuscript paper. I can see they only have four staves on each and no apparent titles or other text. I guess if you are a proper musician you only need to see the notes.

The pieces of paper seem to make the band members chuckle. "Fine by me," says Keyboards. They do not seem worried that these scraps have to keep them going for five to ten minutes. On the strength of his reading of the music, Bass leans his giant instrument against the wall and selects his electric bass. He plugs in, giving the PA its second major challenge of the evening.

Trumpet puts down his prized silvery Yamaha and pulls an electric guitar from the duffle. He is a tall one and it looks like a toy. He gets the band's attention and performs an elaborate pantomime of turning the volume way down before he plugs in. He seems to assume it is tuned OK despite a ride in the back of a car. Maybe it does not matter too much with this number.

Bass pipes up: "What key is it?" he asks, studying his paper, where there is no clue. Trumpet has to think a second or two. "Kind of G Minor," he eventually offers. Drums nods sagely like it makes a difference to him.

Trumpet (waving his guitar) gestures for Drums to kick things off, which he does with sharp raps with a stick on the side of his snare. I note the band have not even had their first free drink yet. Surely asking a jazz band to start a session on a cold night in an unfamiliar venue without any kind of mind-altering substance is a form of cruelty. Despite this Keyboards starts a catchy riff and I realise we are into the old Booker T and the MG's tune "Green Onions".

The old pop number is an odd one for a jazz band to play but I find myself rejoicing that they started with something simple. Even the very best jazz band can be awful at the start of the first number, especially if brass or woodwind are involved. A trumpeter's lips are cold and dry, a sax player's teeth cannot seem to engage with the reed. A guitar is a perfectly reasonable cop-out.

The OAPs in the audience, even me, are starting to sway to the organ when the first guitar chord rings out. I expect to hear false teeth dropping to the floor and I really should be well past joking about things like that. There are rules about this famous introduction; the isolated chord has to be as loud and short as possible and although the guitar must be very much his third or fourth instrument, it's clear that Mr Trumpet really knows how to play this one. Under cover of organ he has turned the volume up to ten (maybe eleven!) and the chord when he strikes it sounds like sheet steel in a chain saw. Just how it should be.

It is rarely used but I know "Onions" to be a great vehicle for improvised solos and the band are itching to get on to that part. Trumpet swings his guitar around behind him and retrieves his silver Yamaha. He licks his lips. I know Drums' playing reasonably well and he is never showy but his role, especially in a configuration like this, is crucial. He is an irritant. Hopefully, he is the piece of grit which produces the pearl. When a soloist is running out of steam it is his job to say, with his drums, *you just can't stop NOW!*

Trumpet begins a solo, probably the first of its kind to ever grace a number like "Green Onions". It is nice but it is not going anywhere and, horror of horrors, he looks like he is about to turn and give 'The Nod' to Keyboards, passing on the baton. Drums decides to take control and executes a drum roll which unmistakably means: *Sorry, too soon, do it again.*

Trumpet looks miffed. He is the leader of the band, dammit. But he responds and finishes the next sequence by unpacking an unlikely chord into even more improbable sequences of notes in higher and higher registers. It is as if he is a ballistic missile which has left the ground with no idea how, or even if, he will ever get down again. Fortunately, Keyboards has followed him into orbit and they swap improbabilities engagingly for a while. Bass, normally very conservative, is up there to, playing a kind of descant of the original organ riff and somehow holding things together.

Drums launched them and he has to bring them down. He seems to know how. First, he gets them back to strict tempo then, at the end of his most extravagant snare drum flourish so far and much ado with cymbals, they all hit the ground together in perfect lock step. We are back to the original catchy theme, as if we had never been in any kind of peril. There is spontaneous applause from an appreciative audience.

When this happens in a band which is well warmed up it is wonderful. In an opening number it is little short of miraculous.

Trumpet returns to his small but lethal guitar and delivers some more of those shattering chords, ending abruptly on the last. Another difficult manoeuvre when a band is running hot.

The applause is at an unheard of volume for a first number. For some reason I feel a little tearful. I cannot wait for the next one.

VEGETABLE REVENGE
Alan Mackenzie

All he was conscious of was the blackness. Not simply the black of the dark when you wake up at night with your eyes closed nor the deep blackness of a nocturnal countryside with no street lighting. No, this was a preternatural black, a black hole where there was simply no light, no colour, no definition of anything. He thought he was conscious – cogito ergo sum after all but even of this he could not be sure. He could, of course, be dead and in some sort of purgatory before assignment to heaven or hell. And yet he could hear himself breathing and he could feel his eyelids open and close. But there was no difference to the blackness. He seemed to be lying down but had no feeling below the neck. Did he still have his body? Or was he in some sort of suspended animation with just his head remaining. He sent instructions to his muscles to move his mouth, but nothing seemed to happen. He tried to make a noise with similar negative results.

He heard the air rustling quietly around him and vague sounds which might have been someone speaking but he could discern no words, no conversation as such. He was in a complete limbo. He felt a sense of panic rising. Was he perhaps in a protracted process of dying? Gradually his efforts to comprehend his situation became too much and he lost consciousness and fell into a deep sleep.

After a time, he seemed to be awake again. He could not say how long he had been absent. A minute? An hour? A day or a week? In that black hole there were no reference points. The space-time continuum had been reduced to a singularity where he had only minute perceptions of things outside his universe. And yet from the cloud of murmurs around him he began to catch hold of sounds which he recognised as words or phrases. His head was moved sideways, and he heard a deep, molasses-sweet voice speaking to him. He heard "out of here" and "Mr Spencer". Was that his name? Was somebody trying to get him out wherever he was? His head was moved back again, and he felt something being inserted in his mouth and a cool and refreshing liquid coursing down his throat. If he was dying, then someone was clearly trying to keep him alive.

After another interval of sleep, he awoke to the sound of several voices either side of his head. The molasses voice – this must be a nurse – had been joined by one lighter and more authoritative. He heard "Mr Spencer" again – this must be his own name. Then he heard "medication" and "vegetative". Clearly this was a doctor and he felt unaccountably cheered by his small success at understanding the concept of nurse and doctor. Then there was another rather booming voice in his left ear which uttered the word "investigation". Were they, whoever they were, trying to find out why he was there?

He slept and another time passed. It could have been a decade, a century, or a millennium as far as he knew. Then he heard voices again. This time there were many. He could not see but his hearing could distinguish the differences clearly. The voices he recognised as those of the nurse, the doctor and the investigator gave way to a crisp, meticulously enunciated baritone who was obviously in charge. He appeared to be laying down conditions, steps to take, Rubicons to cross. He heard "life support", "tragic" and "cannot continue". What could not continue? Then, suddenly, he heard a new voice, metallic but not unpleasant like a silver spoon tinkling on a cup of tea. More importantly he realised with an emotion akin to joy that he recognised it. He remembered the voice. He knew that he knew the person. If only he could recall who exactly she was. Yes, that was it, it was a woman he knew very well. He tried in vain to extract from the trillions of neurones and synapses in his brain one element of recognition – a face, a smell, a touch – but nothing came. He gradually sank back into the blackness.

The voices came again, and he surfaced with a start from his black hole. This time there seemed to be a sense of urgency in the words being used. The doctor said, "the time has come" and "turn off". Little Miss molasses said "cryin' shame" while the investigator said "accident" three times. There seemed to be a long discussion until finally the silver spoon said, "willing to sign" and then a mobile phone suddenly rang. It had the ring tone of You Are My Heart's Delight from the Land of Smiles. In that one instant the black hole exploded, his eyes could see and with a sense of horror he remembered everything.

The phone belonged to his wife Eleanor and it was she who had pushed him down the stairs when he had found out about her affair. As he lay with a neck twisted and presumably dying it was she who had called her lover on the phone. He remembered hearing her say "thank God he's dead". It was she who put him in the black hole and was about to sign his death sentence.

With his sight miraculously restored he looked around to see the bodies of the voices he had heard. They all appeared immobilised in surprise. Molasses nurse looked in wonder while the doctor and the head of the Department were the picture of consternation that their negative diagnoses had been proved wrong. The detective constable was frozen in the act of marking the end of his investigation in a notebook. And, finally, there was Eleanor – dearly beloved Eleanor, Eleanor with the silver spoon voice, Eleanor his wife whom he had loved for 30 years – in a state that could only be described as catatonic clutching her mobile phone with the wonderful ringing tones of Richard Tauber.

He smiled, turned his head to the detective and with an enormous effort managed to say, "I need to talk to you alone".

MERCY
Richard Clifton

PC Sophia Russo should have been grateful for the opportunity she had been afforded this week. She had pleaded to be given some experience which would support her application for a move into plain clothes and this was the best they could do. She was to shadow DI Baxter on a "special investigation" he was undertaking.

She knew Baxter quite well because he had an office close to her desk. He was an amiable old fool now only months from retirement. He was not exactly at the cutting edge of current investigations; in fact, she had the distinct impression he had been assigned "light duties" running up to his big day. She might have even liked him if he could have remembered her name and refrained for addressing her as "young lady". She was twenty-seven.

If she was to be his effective PA, that probably meant bag-carrying, digging out records from the archives and other general drudgery. She knew better than to complain at this stage in her career and resigned herself to a boring week.

Reporting to his office on Monday morning, she felt as though she had walked into one of the smoking enclaves in the car park. Since smoking was forbidden anywhere inside the station the thick fog was clearly coming from Baxter himself. She guessed he had been closeted in the gents for a while, taking on a day's supply of nicotine. Baxter looked up as she walked in, appearing briefly like a rabbit caught in car headlights.

"PC Russo, sir" she said. "I'm assigned to you this week."

"My dear young lady," said Baxter, clearly not remembering a thing. "of course, you are. I've been really looking forward to it!"

Smarmy old sod thought Sophia.

"No time to lose," said Baxter, recovering quickly and handing her a buff folder. "Skim through these notes and come back in half an hour. We're going out to see the scene of the ... whatever it turns out to be, this morning."

Sophia took the folder back to her desk while Baxter went in search of coffee.

He passed by her desk a few minutes later with a steaming mug. "I think you'll find it quite interesting," he said, before returning to his office and putting his feet up.

The case was sad but unremarkable. A man of fifty-five had died of motor neurone disease, leaving a wife and two grown-up children, the latter now living abroad. A note from the station medical officer was included remarking that cause of death was probably lack of oxygen, a common outcome in such cases. This had been confirmed in a later autopsy. There were no suspicious circumstances indicating violent asphyxia, such as broken blood vessels in the eyes or soft tissues of the face. Sophia was left wondering why this case was still a matter of concern to the police.

Her half-hour was up but Baxter looked as though he was fast asleep in his office. She took another twenty minutes on the internet, researching MND and the drugs, equipment and other palliatives used to treat sufferers.

She was making notes as Baxter lurched out of his office, rattling a set of car keys. "I've got my usual car," he said. "Do you mind driving? Feeling a bit under the weather this morning."

"No problem, sir" she said brightly. So, it was bag-carrying, research, general drudgery and driving.

It was easy to see why this particular unmarked Vauxhall Astra was regarded as Baxter's. The other officers probably would not go near it. It reeked of tobacco and was full of his personal junk, which he scooped off the passenger seat and threw in the back as he got in. To Sophia's surprise he was up to programming the satnav.

"Ok, let's go, young lady" he said. "We don't need lights and sirens today." He winked at her. One more "young lady" and she thought she would have to punch him in the eye. For the moment, she refrained.

"The Chief Super passes quite a few of these cases to me," he confided as they drove. "I've become a bit of an expert. They seem like death from natural causes, but you never know, and they have to be thoroughly checked out."

"Do they?"

Baxter looked at her sharply. "Yes, they do, young lady! Life and death are in the hands of almighty God alone, and woe betide anyone who takes them into their own hands."

"Yes, sir" she said in as flat a voice as possible. She would never have figured Baxter as a member of the God squad. She cancelled the long-overdue punch in the eye a second time when she remembered her grandmother would almost certainly have had the same view, but then she was a sweet old lady, not an oaf.

Ten minutes later they arrived at a large fifties' semi in one of the leafier parts of town. Mrs Beswick, a very tired-looking woman, was surprised to see the police again but let them in and started to make tea.

Baxter accepted tea and a ginger nut and was at his smarmy best, saying there were just a few i's to be dotted and t's crossed in the statement and that would be the end of it.

"... and perhaps I could take a look at the breathing equipment your husband was using before his death, "said Sophia. "Is it still around?"

Baxter gave her a sharp look again. "Yes, that too," he said.

Sophia studied Mrs Beswick's face for any reaction to mention of the equipment but detected nothing. She just looked resigned.

"It's all in the garage," she said.

Sophia sat quietly as Baxter went through Mrs Beswick's statement. There was not much to it. The unfortunate man had been expected to last a few more weeks but release had come early, and she had found him one morning, peacefully dead with no signs of struggle. As Mrs Beswick was speaking Baxter, from time to time, gave her what he obviously thought was a penetrating stare. Reading her soul, no doubt.

Afterwards Sophia and Baxter went through the garden to the garage, following Mrs Beswick's directions.

"We don't really need to do this," said Baxter. "I can read people and I know she's on the level."

You arsehole, thought Sophia. "But it'll look good in the report," she said.

"Yes, of course," said Baxter.

They found the oxygen cylinder in the garage along with various tools and fittings. Baxter sat on a stool while Sophia familiarized herself with the equipment, which conformed closely to diagrams she had seen on the internet.

She unscrewed the valve on the cylinder about a quarter turn and was alarmed by a massive release of oxygen. Glancing at Baxter she saw to her horror that he had just lit a cigarette. She expected it to turn into a blazing firework in his mouth as the oxygen reached it. There would be a certain funny side to that, but she did not want to be the one to rush her boss to A&E on their first assignment. Actually, nothing happened.

"Hey, my fag's gone out," said Baxter.

"Better not light up while I'm messing about with pure oxygen," she said.
"No, of course not," said Baxter.

Sophia looked at the small pressure gauge on the side of the oxygen bottle. She couldn't remember exactly what she had read on the 'net, but it might be two or three times the normal operating pressure employed in oxygen used in the home. She made a note of it.

"Well there's plenty in the cylinder," she said after some thought. "I guess that's it."

As they walked back to the house, she considered telling Baxter that Mr Beswick had almost certainly not died of natural causes. Who knows, she might be in plain clothes in a matter of months.

"You go on," she said. "I've left my notebook in the garage." Actually, it was safe in her pocket.

"Never leave your notebook lying around," said Baxter, wagging his finger. He would never know how close he came to that punch in the eye.

Sophia rushed back to the garage and opened the valve on the cylinder, just a little way. She left it hissing.

It occurred to her that she was destroying evidence but, on the other hand, an over-pressurized gas cylinder was a bomb waiting to go off. It might have blown the garage apart. She was merely making it safe.

Baxter was in the kitchen apologizing for the intrusion when she got back to the house. The case was closed as far as he was concerned. Thank goodness for that man's faultless intuition.

After the case was formally closed Sophia spent some time researching nitrogen anoxia. It had been proposed as a method of execution in the state of Alabama but rejected on the grounds that it was not sufficiently unpleasant.

They decided to stick with Old Sparky the electric chair, which was cruel and unusual enough to keep all right-thinking citizens happy.

She thought about trying to find out how Mrs Beswick got her nitrogen. There are numerous industrial uses such as filling bags of ready-made salad. Perhaps she knew someone who did that. Filling from an industrial supply would certainly explain the over-pressure. Sophia decided to forget about the whole thing.

What Mrs Beswick must have known is that breathing pure nitrogen for any length of time it is just like breathing air – without the oxygen. The carbon dioxide which causes feelings of suffocation is purged from the lungs in the normal way and the lack of oxygen brings on peaceful sleep, followed swiftly by painless death.

LOL

Alan Mackenzie

John had not wanted to retire. He enjoyed his job as the chief accountant of Metal Works Ltd. He had been told that some people thought accountancy was boring, but he revelled in the precision of the figures, the poetic accuracy of the debits and credits, the calligraphic beauty of his financial annexes. He even enjoyed the predictability of his daily commute – a five minute walk from his house in Acacia Road to get the number 13 bus at 8:10 AM which dropped him off just outside the firm's offices a quarter of an hour later. He would say good morning to Anne the receptionist, a buxom redhead with an infrequent smile who always seemed to be doing something with her nails. He would climb the short flight of stairs to his domain which was grandiloquently called the Finance Division. In fact, it was just three small offices – his, his deputy's (Samantha) and his clerk's (Ron). He would have a cup of tea at 10:30 and lunch from 12:30 to 1:30. At 5 o'clock he would pack up and return home for tea at 6 which his wife, Phyllis, had prepared. It was a perfect if rather boring routine.

Phyllis and John had no children. This was not the result of a conscious decision. It was simply a fact of their lives together which they had accepted. John, however, had one passion and that was the stars. Some years ago, he had bought a second-hand telescope on a whim in a local boot sale. He had taken it home, cleaned it up and looked out one evening at the night sky and had discovered the universe. While Phyllis spent her evenings phoning her friends or engaging in social media, he would survey the galaxies and make precise notes on the moon and planets, the movements of stars and their luminosity. He had bought bigger and better telescopes so that now he could see far into the centre of the Milky Way. He had even built a small shed at the bottom of the garden as his "observatory" with a window on the roof through which he could extend his telescope. He would spend most evenings and weekends there in a rapt contemplation of the cosmos which was akin to some mystical trance.

But now he had to retire. Steve, his boss, and the chief executive of Metal Works Ltd, had been very nice about it. After all John had worked for the company for 35 years and, at the age of 67, it was time for him to enjoy life a bit while he could and make the most of the generous pension package the company was providing. John had protested politely that he was fully prepared, indeed keen, to continue working. Steve appreciated that and all the years of trustworthy and reliable service that John had given to the firm. However, retirement was something to embrace not resist. It would give both John and Phyllis the opportunity to do things they had not been able to do before. It was true that Steve was not going to replace John when he left but Samantha was quite capable of doing the work and what with the downturn in markets and Chinese competition the firm had to look to tightening its belt.

On the Friday afternoon of his retirement John was given a modest farewell reception in the firm's executive room. Steve gave a speech praising John's major "contribution" over many years and the staff raised their glasses of cheap prosecco and sang "for he's a jolly good fellow" out of tune. John returned home in time for tea – mushrooms on toast.

Those first weeks of retirement were difficult for John. While Phyllis had her coffee mornings with friends, her weekly yoga classes and meetings of the Women's Institute, John – who had never been interested in cooking, sports, gardening, or DIY – missed his work. He found little consolation in pottering about the house or reading those books he had never read but had always promised to do so. And although he knew he could talk to Phyllis on those rare occasions when she was present and not on the phone or Facebook, Snapchat, WhatsApp, Instagram or Twitter exchanging yet more banalities with some friend or relative, he realised quite soon that he did not want to. After all, what would he talk to her about? The only consolation he found was in looking at the stars every evening.

Phyllis was not worried about John. She saw that he had nothing to do and that he was somewhat disconsolate, but she also knew that he was strong and reliable. He might be in the doldrums for the moment, but he would snap out of it in due course. Her friends bolstered her optimism by assuring her that this was a phase all men went through after retirement. She should be patient and think of things to do together – perhaps a holiday would help.

It was a month after his retirement that Phyllis suggested a week's holiday in Spain.

"Alicante would be nice, don't you think?" She had paused with a finger over the phone as she composed a message to her friend Cynthia who had recently opened a hairdressing salon.

"What?" John was engrossed in a book about the sun and trying to conceive of a temperature of 15,000,000°C which was apparently the heat at its centre.

"Just for a few days. Lovely climate this time of year. There's this nice hotel and we can get a cheap flight from Gatwick. What do you think?" Her phone buzzed with yet another message from her brother, Ed, who was going through a difficult divorce.

"I suppose so. Whatever you like, dear." John was trying to get his head around the physics of the seething mass of hydrogen and helium at the centre of the solar system which had been burning for billions of years and had given rise to life on earth. Had fostered the development of plants and animals over countless eons. Had created by some unbelievable act of serendipity the conditions that gave rise to civilisation on a minor planet that just happened to be in a Goldilocks orbit. Had nurtured the rise of thought and culture in an unremarkable animal species known as homo sapiens. And had ultimately nurtured the technological advances which enabled Phyllis's phone to buzz on the breakfast table with an email from her sister.

"I'll go ahead and book it then. Oh, look John. I see that Pam has finally decided to go ahead and marry her Tom. You remember him, don't you?" She did not expect John to reply and, in any event, he would have had difficulty distinguishing Tom from all the other boyfriends her sister had had since her last divorce.

Despite the evident lack of enthusiasm on John's part, Phyllis busied herself with booking the hotel and the flight to Alicante. Two weeks later they drove to Gatwick, boarded the low-cost flight to Alicante and within five hours were unpacking in an elegantly appointed bedroom on the twelfth floor of a four-star hotel. Their room had a glorious view of the Mediterranean and John spent some time impassively contemplating the sun as it began to set over an impossibly azure sea.

"Isn't this nice, John? I must just send a few messages. Cynthia and Pam would just love this." Her fingers pecked rapidly at her mobile phone like some starving chicken. John muttered something and went out onto the balcony with his mobile phone. The city was set out just like a tourist postcard below him and he could see the beaches and catch the glint of sunlight on the sea. It was too perfect, too beautiful, he thought. He, too, tapped briefly on his phone, climbed onto the wall of the balcony and with one last contemplation of the setting sun launched himself into the air. It took only a few seconds for his body to fall and crack onto the patio below. He died instantly, of course, and his blood rapidly seeped around his body and created a halo around his head like the corona around the sun.

Phyllis did not hear the sound of the body hitting the patio nor the panicked shouts of the hotel guests and staff. She was too busy sending messages on her phone. Suddenly, however, she recalled with a start what John had muttered as he went on to the balcony. He had said "I'm just going for a cigarette". John had never smoked. As if in slow motion she moved to the balcony window. She stepped out transfixed not by the glorious view but by the realisation that John had disappeared. She looked down to the ground floor patio where his body lay spread-eagled in a growing pool of blood and began to scream.

It was at that point that her phone buzzed again. It was a message from John. It read simply "At last I am free. LOL. John." Her screams gave way to sobs as she looked at John's last communication. His last brief missive on this world had been to send her lots of love. Or was it laughing out loud?

FAKE NEWS
Alan Mackenzie

It was Christmas Eve. Pennsylvania Avenue in Washington DC was being swept by the typical winter winds from the north. There was the usual number of homeless squatting under blankets in front of the White House. The police would sweep them away at regular intervals, but the hardy souls would always return in the hope of begging a few dollars from passers-by. As the daylight faded, the thermometer fell and snowflakes began twinkling in the dark sky, a surprising number of Santa Clauses appeared on the street clanking their collection boxes. Some were kosher and had official charity badges to prove it. Others were clearly on the make, their red-and-white costumes smudged with the grime of trying to make a living in this capital of the free world. The snow became thicker and towards 6 o'clock in the evening the traffic dissipated, and a hush fell over the capital.

In the White House itself it was business as usual. It might be Christmas Eve but the process of government of, by and for the people could not stop for Christ's birth. True, there were drinks here and there in the offices but the Marines still stood guard; interns, staffers and politicians strode purposefully from one meeting to another; computers, phones and fax machines still buzzed, trilled and clacked away in their endless, and ultimately vain, attempt to keep up with the information flow.

It was about 10 o'clock that James Trevelyan III, the White House chief of staff and Jim to his friends, decided it was time to head home. He had had his last debriefing with the president who had retired to bed at his usual time of 9:30 PM. He called for his car to pick him up and drive him to his townhouse just outside Washington where he was looking forward to joining his family for two days off. He sat back at his desk and, for the first time in many weeks, sighed with relief. At his age (he was seventy-one next year) the pace of life was gradually taking its toll. He would see out the current president's term but would then retire gracefully to the ranch he had bought in Texas. He reflected that the current administration had managed to accomplish much in its first two years. Unemployment was down, economic growth and the dollar was up, most minorities had been placated and the world seemed a much more peaceful place with fewer wars and a surprising rapprochement with the hitherto implacable enemies of the USA. Okay, there were still some terrorist incidents and a few genocides here and there but in general he thought the world was in a better place. He was happy and proud to be an American.

He stood up and was about to pack his briefcase when there was a knock on the door and his chief aide, Patrick O'Halloran, rushed in in a state of agitation.

"Chief, we have a situation."

"What sort of situation?" Jim had difficulty disguising his irritation. This was after all Christmas Eve.

"You're not going to believe this, Sir, but the communication centre has just reported that we are under attack."

"You've got to be kidding me. Under attack? What sort of attack? Who is being attacked? Who the hell launches an attack on Christmas Eve?"

"We are still trying to get confirmation of details, but it appears that someone, somewhere and for some reason has just launched a hundred nuclear missiles with targets assessed as being on mainland USA."

Jim took in a deep breath. He could not believe this. It had to be some prankster; some hoaxer determined to ruin his Christmas. Either that or the computer systems had gone haywire. It was inconceivable that any of the likely culprits in the world would or, indeed, could initiate such an attack. Only that afternoon he had spoken on the phone to the president of the Russian Federation and parted with a cheerful "Happy Christmas". And he had sent a Christmas card with the picture of a panda to the president of China.

"Jesus, Pat! This simply can't be true. Has DOD declared any DEFCON? What's the news from NORAD? And how much time have we got?"

"We are still working on getting all the players involved, Sir, but the best estimate seems to be that we have about thirty minutes."

"Well, you'd better work a damn sight faster because I'm not missing my Christmas day for some God almighty fuck-up through Facebook, Twitter or Google. You know the drill, Pat. I want the VP, Secretary of State, DOD, Chief of the General Staff, NORAD, CIA, FBI and any other acronym you can think of to be either present in the bunker or on the phone within five minutes. We also need to set up a press release and a presidential address if this is real. I'll get the president."

"Arrangements are already made, Sir." Pat scuttled off to get the latest information as the corridors of power suddenly filled with people rushing to find out what the hell was going on.

Jim got to the presidential suite within two minutes and accompanied by two Marine guards, entered the anteroom. The president, Charles P. McLaughlin IV, scion of a Republican political dynasty which went back a hundred and fifty years, was already dressed and muttering expletives at what he saw as an unnecessary disturbance.

"What the fuck is all this about Jim?"

Jim briefed the president as they descended into the bunker under the White House past the saluting guards and the bomb blast doors into the complex of the communication centre and the briefing room. The president nodded to the fifty or so people and sat down at the head of the roundtable surrounded by numerous computer screens showing satellite pictures and computer graphics of the world and, in detail, the USA.

"Well, ladies and gentlemen, I guess we have an unprecedented situation here. We have only a few minutes to decide what to do." He turned to the marine guard on his right who held the briefcase with the nuclear button which only the president could press. "We'll start with a debrief from the Secretary of State."

"Mr President, we now have confirmation from NORAD and the DOD that our satellite system has identified 96 intercontinental ballistic missiles on their way to targets on mainland USA with an ETA of 17 minutes. Our anti-missile defence is capable of taking out most of these, but this still leaves some with a real chance of reaching their targets. We estimate that San Francisco, Chicago, Alabama, New York, and Washington are likely to be in the line of fire with casualties in the tens of millions. All emergency services are already on alert, we are at DEFCON 4 and the helicopter is on standby to take you to Air Force One." Mrs Brightman paused meaningfully. "If there is time."

"Mr President, unbelievable though it sounds all the missiles appear to have been launched in a coordinated attack from China, Russia, France, UK, Pakistan, India and North Korea but our contacts in all these nations except Korea deny any such move. No other nation or entity has claimed any responsibility." General Arthur D. Anderson, Chief of the General Staff, was pale and grim.

"Jesus Christ, are you sure this is real, General? This must be a hoax, some global cyberattack from an anti-US wacko. I mean, I know the UK Prime Minister doesn't like me, but I got on fine with the Queen at the Palace...." The President's voice tailed off. He fervently hoped that this was some ghastly hoax but feared he was clutching at straws. After all, his administration had invested trillions of dollars in defence and so everything pointed to the attack being a horrible reality.

"Mr President, we have run all the checks possible and our cyber defence capabilities are unparalleled. I'm afraid there is no doubt that this is real."

The room fell silent as they contemplated the picture of the USA with the data from the satellites showing the lines of approach of the missiles. The Chief of Staff and of the room and whispered in the President's ear. All could now hear the muffled sound of the blast doors of the bunker being closed.

"We have no time to evacuate and no time to respond and we don't even know who is attacking us. Ladies and gentlemen, there is only one thing we can do and that is pray." The President put his hands together and bowed his head. The assembled company followed suit, some with a forceful conviction and others with an embarrassed hesitancy.

Suddenly, all the computer screens and lights in the briefing room went out. In the pitch dark you could hear the gasps of in-drawn breath. Was this the nuclear shock? Was this really the end of days? Four Marine guards automatically surrounded the president in his chair prepared to die in defence of their Chief. After a very long minute the lights and computer screens came on again but, this time, they were blank. No pictures of the world or the USA, no data and no missile flight lines. Just a blank, white canvas upon which appeared gradually the words "Surprise! Surprise!" And then "Happy Christmas!" with the emoji of a laughing Santa.

SOCIAL MURDER
Alan Mackenzie

Emma was late for work yet again. She had had a late night out with Hugh and Elliott in their local pub in Finsbury Park and, as she scrambled to get dressed to the accompaniment of an irritating buzz from the alarm clock in her ears, she bitterly regretted the last three glasses of Merlot the night before. Snatching her handbag, she virtually tumbled down the stairs from her bedsit and ran all the way to the tube station where she just managed to get the 9.05 to central London. Changing at Warren Street for the Northern line she got to Charing Cross just after 10 and got to her office in the Ministry of Defence library in Whitehall twenty minutes later. She felt hot, flustered, and grimy and, with a deep sigh, prepared herself to face the roistering she would undoubtedly get from her boss Mrs Warren.

"Emma! How nice of you to pop in! We are so grateful you've managed to find time to come to work." Mrs Warren, Enid to her very few friends, was a fifty-six-year-old who lived in Wembley Park and had devoted over thirty years of her life to running the archives of the MOD central library with terrifying professionalism. During that time, she had also sharpened her tongue to a razor which could kill. There was allegedly a Mr Warren although no one had seen him, and it was generally rumoured that he had been buried in the back garden of Enid's house many years ago having previously been verbally savaged by his wife.

Mrs Warren beckoned Emma to follow her into her office where she sat down behind an imposing oak desk and folded her hands as though in prayer.

"Mrs Warren, I'm so sorry. You see, the water in the bath overflowed this morning and I had to clean it up. It was already going down the stairs to the next floor. It won't happen again." Emma knew she was blustering and realised too late that she had already use this excuse.

Mrs Warren licked her lips in anticipation and paraphrased Oscar Wilde. "To have one bath overflow in a week is unfortunate. To have two sounds like carelessness." She paused and relished Emma's discomfiture. "I wonder whether you are really cut out for an office job and whether plumbing might not be a better career path." Oh, the joy and satisfaction of sarcasm when you are talking to someone thirty-eight years your junior! Emma reddened with anger and frustration which was largely directed to herself but which she managed to translate into a profound dislike of her boss.

"Well, you'd better get on. Archives wait for no man or woman and we've already wasted half a day." Evidently dismissed, Emma turned to go when Mrs Warren added "If it happens again, Emma, I shall have no choice but to take further action." Emma mouthed silently "bloody old bitch" as she went to her own office which was more a cupboard unfortunately adjacent to her boss. She sat down, took out her phone and vented her anger in a somewhat vitriolic Facebook posting to Hugh and Elliott who, at that very moment, were turning up for work late to the Amazon warehouse in Wembley Park. The two 20-year-olds received even less empathy from their boss, Fred, who had sacked them on the spot and sent them packing with a stream of expletives and a tirade of invective about the general fecklessness of the younger generation.

"Bloody sod! I could kill the bastard. How can he sack us just like that? There must be some law or other against that. I'm going to ask my dad." Hugh's father was a police constable and knew something about the law although his expertise on employment legislation was unlikely to be extensive.

Elliott was counting his money. "I've got twenty quid left till the end of the month and the rent's due at the end of the week. I can't see Mr Samuelson giving me any slack. At this rate I'll have to go back and live with my mum." Mr Samuelson, their landlord, charged the lads £800 a month for two small rooms and a shared bathroom in a dingy terraced house a stone's throw from Finsbury Park tube station. While Hugh was a dropout from university (much to the disappointment of his father) where he had been studying in a very dilatory fashion business management, Elliott had left school at sixteen and had had a variety of jobs none of which had lasted more than six months. They were both likeable lads with engaging personalities. But with every passing month it seemed to both of them that society was determined to put them in their place.

As they looked glumly at each other, Hugh's phone pinged. It was the message from Emma. "Looks like Emma's got the same problems with her boss. We may as well meet up tonight to drown our sorrows."

Having agreed to meet Hugh and Elliott at the World's End in Finsbury Park at 7.30 Emma arrived early and seated herself at a table near the entrance to the pub. Hugh was the first to arrive followed shortly by Elliott accompanied by a slight young man with rather greasy black hair dressed in a black leather jerkin and a vivid red shirt whom she did not recognise and who was not introduced.

Hugh bought a round of drinks, beer for the boys and a white wine for Emma and they began to excoriate jointly the ruling class for whom they worked.

"There are times when I wish you could kill the bitch. She is always looking down on me and picking at everything I do. Just because I've been late on a few occasions." Emma was feeling a keen sense of injustice, totally unjustified of course but she could not see that.

"Ah, they're all the same. Give them a bit of power and all they want to do is screw the poor sods working for them." Elliott grumbled bitterly over his beer. Hugh grumbled his agreement "It's the capitalist system, isn't it? It is always the same – the rich get richer while the poor are gradually ground into the dust. That's why I gave up business management." Hugh had read some extracts from Das Kapital and fancied himself as an expert on Marxism.

"I'd like to boil her in oil, the bloody bitch." Emma was getting carried away as she applied herself to a second glass of wine. "I'd like to see Fred crushed under a hundred Amazon pallets. Workers of the world unite!" Hugh slurped his beer and his eyes grew bright at the thought of meting out a just retribution.

"And I'd put old Samuelson in the electric chair for screwing us over the rent." Elliott had a brief image of the portly figure of Mr Samuelson writhing in agony as 20,000 volts coursed through his body.

"What do you think, Luke? Do you think we should get rid of'em all? Have a purge on the ruling classes? We could reduce the population of the world and achieve a socialist Nirvana all in one go." Hugh was laughing as all three turned their eyes on the young man in the black jerkin and red shirt.

"I dunno. I s'pose they all deserve it. I couldn't really say. The problem is getting it done and then getting away with it." Luke took a long draught of his beer and smiled as he put down his glass. They all laughed together, ordered another round, and went on to discuss the latest episode of Strictly Come Dancing.

The four of them left the pub at closing time, Hugh and Elliott having exhausted their spare cash and Emma nursing yet another headache but this time it was the fault of the sauvignon. As they said their goodbyes promising to meet at the weekend, they noticed that Luke had simply disappeared.

Emma swore off the drink for the next two days and managed to get into work on time. As she arrived on Friday morning, she saw two policemen outside the office and a huddle of people at Mrs Warren's door muttering in subdued tones.

"What's going on, Frances?" Emma addressed the receptionist who managed to look both surprised and worried. "It's Mrs Warren. She's dead."

"Oh my God! You must be joking. What happened?"

"Happened last night apparently. They say it was her husband. Poured boiling chip oil all over her and she died of shock. He's denying it of course. Claims he was at his bowling club. The police are still, as they say, pursuing their investigations but he's under arrest all the same."

Emma sat down at her desk pale with shock. She looked over at Mrs Warren's office and the empty chair from which her now deceased boss had looked ferociously on a daily basis over her underlings. Yes, she hated the old biddy but could not wish such a horrible death on anyone. At midday, the director of the library decided to close the offices and told everyone to go home.

Emma sent a message to Hugh and Elliott and arrived at seven at the World's End. She was nursing a gin and tonic when Hugh came in and said excitedly "You'll never guess what's happened!"

"What?"

"It's Fred. You know that bloody old git we were working for at Amazon. The one that fired us. He died this morning. Fifty pallets of Fairy Liquid were pushed over on him by a lorry reversing. Crushed him to death. I can't believe it. I need a drink."

Hugh bought his pint of beer and listened as Emma recounted the news of her boss's own death.

"Bloody coincidence, isn't it?" Hugh looked nonplussed at the implausibility of two such accidents occurring one after the other so soon after they had talked jokingly about the very same modes of death. Just then Elliott walked in and announced that Mr Samuelson had sadly passed away the evening before. He had been found in his bath with an electric fire in the water still plugged into the mains. He had been electrocuted.

All three of them looked at each other and simultaneously swore "Jesus Christ".

"Bloody hell." said Elliott "All we need is Luke to come in and announce another death. I'm beginning to think there's something strange going on."

"How do you know Luke?" Emma looked quizzically at Hugh.

"Never met him before. I thought he was your friend." Both turned to Elliott. "Well, I'd never met him before the other night. He was standing outside the pub and said he was a friend of Hugh's and that's when we came in together."

At that instant, all three phones pinged and they each looked at their screens. They all saw the same message "Be careful what you wish for! LOL Luke."

THE MESSAGE
Richard Clifton

Once again, I am walking the beach alone, not long after dawn. I follow the retreating tide, where the drying sand is firm and easy to walk on. This is the best combination of time and tide; it is just before breakfast and the sea is as far out as it goes. Over the years I have made a study of the local tide tables and I know when these special days fall due. The weather is another important factor of course, but today is clear and already bright so all three of my boxes are ticked. It is very chilly for March though. I feel the cold much more these days. I am startled by the pitter-pat of running feet behind me. Two greyhounds, or whippets perhaps, come by at unbelievable speed, leaving tiny, perfect pawprints in the pristine sand. I turn to see their owner, a solitary female figure nearly half a mile back along the beach. A faint whistle stops them in their tracks and they race back to mama with even greater speed. They acknowledge me briefly as they pass with a sideways look. "Sorry can't stop," they seem to say. I normally turn for home at this point, just before the next headland, but last night's storm has turned up quite a lot of flotsam and I stick with it in case something interesting turns up. Something floating about twenty yards out catches my eye. A bottle. It is an ordinary-looking clear glass bottle and probably contained gin or something. It seems to be coming in to shore, so I await its arrival. Losing patience, I wade out into the icy water to pick it up but my timing is wrong, A returning wave takes it out to sea again, but I get a good look at it. It seems to have a rolled-up paper inside. Could that be a message in the bottle? How exciting. The bottle stays about thirty yards out, bobbing in the waves. It moves in a complex circulating path, but generally along the coast. Fascinated, I follow it. At the rocky headland the bottle, caught in a greater circulation, starts to move further out to sea. It seems hopeless but I think perhaps it will become lodged in the tumbled boulders and maybe I can grab it. I clamber onto the rocks gingerly. I am not quite so agile as I used to be. It takes a while to make my way over the rocks, but I keep the bottle in view. It is going nowhere very fast because the tide is on the turn now.

The headland peters out into a profusion of giant rocks. I think they are under water at all but the lowest tides; they are covered in weed like green baize, dry now but probably not for long. I see the bottle bobbing between them and can hear it clinking occasionally as it impacts the weedy stones. The water is quite choppy now; surely the glass will shatter at any time. It is now or never. Casting caution aside I jump from rock to rock. The dry weed provides fairly reliable footing and I soon achieve the rounded boulder adjacent to the bottle. If I lie face down, I can just reach down to the water line and grab it by the neck. That done, and feeling rather exhausted, I make myself comfortable on top of the boulder to examine my prize.

The top is made fully water-tight with duct tape and a great deal of some kind of gunk. It will prove difficult to open but, with growing shock, I realise I do not need to. I find myself quite familiar with the contents and with the handwriting I can see on the loosely rolled note inside. It is my own.

I sit there for some time, my breathing heavy and my heart thumping. It dawns on me that witnessing such an astronomically unlikely event at first hand is actually very frightening. It makes you think just about anything can happen; and maybe there is such a thing as fate. This is how religions start. Think of all the billions of times coincidences do not happen, I am telling myself. It is not working so far. The evidence before me is that I hold, in a rather shaky hand, a bottle I had thrown into the sea myself, not far from here, over forty years previously. Even though I could not have described it during the intervening years, the sight of it now is quite unmistakable. Even now I struggle with the idea.

Surely there must be another explanation, but it does not come to mind. All those years ago my old friend and I had both been dumped by our girlfriends, on the same night. Now I know we had asked for it; back then we were not so understanding. After we drowned our sorrows in the former contents of the bottle I had written some very unpleasant things about those very decent young ladies and launched the defamatory essay into the ocean from the cliff on the other side of the beach. It is difficult to believe the bottle has remained seaworthy all those years. Perhaps it lodged in rocks above high water until the recent storm freed it. Who knows? I smash the bottle and shred the paper inside. I think that is the right thing to do, and long overdue.

Unfortunately, on the way back, I find the returning tide has turned the weedy baize into green glass and I slip on the rocks. My leg is now trapped between the big boulders and I am up to my chest in water. The smaller stones down there, the size of grapefruit, are ground very smooth from rattling around in the waves. They feel surprisingly comfortable, but they hold my leg so very securely. I could no sooner free myself than pull my foot off. Thank goodness I have kept my mobile phone dry. The water seems a lot colder and I am feeling quite weak now. Obviously, I have called the lifeboat people but the signal's not great around here. Sent a text too. No reply yet.

THE LAST WILL AND TESTAMENT OF JOE FULLER
Alan Mackenzie

The news that Joe Fuller had died spread through the village like a thunderclap. It was received with the same level of shock as when George VI died or when John F. Kennedy was assassinated. News in the press of volcanic eruptions in Sumatra, forest fires in Amazonia and the melting of the Greenland ice cap paled into insignificance compared with the demise of the oldest inhabitant of Fulmersham, Bedfordshire, population 367.

Of course, they knew he was old. Just how old was a frequent subject of debate in the Six Bells. Some said ninety-three while others put his age at over one hundred. Since all of his contemporaries had long since shuffled off this mortal coil, there was no one available to confirm categorically any particular age and Joe himself was punctilious in avoiding any discussion of the subject. He was certainly born well before the Second World War during which he served with distinction as evinced by the number of medals he wore every year at the Fulmersham church Armistice Day service. But Joe preferred to consider himself as immortal and, until shortly before his death, strode through the village every morning with his walking stick and a jaunty flat cap bidding good day to everyone he met as though he were the Lord of the Manor greeting his loyal peasants.

He was, indeed, effectively regarded as the patriarch of the village. Everyone knew he was rich – he had apparently owned a successful textile factory, many houses in Bedford and Luton, extensive lands around Fulmersham and, some said, extensive properties abroad. He was also the proud owner of the largest property in Fulmersham – a sprawling Georgian mansion, known as the Manse, with six bedrooms and five acres of grounds including a boathouse by the side of the river Ouse to which he would invite not only his extended family but most of the village for a grand feast and fireworks every Christmas. He was generous with both his time and money, serving on the local parish committee and Rotary club and making regular donations to charities in the region. Since the death of his wife some thirty years before Joe had, in fact, increased his philanthropic activities and had funded a new clubhouse for the village. This was originally intended to be a youth club but since the average age of the village inhabitants was fifty-seven, it had immediately been appropriated by the local WI and Bridge club.

In summary, the passing of Joe Fuller was akin to the extinction of a star in the firmament for the village of Fulmersham. No longer would the villagers see him on his morning constitutional or, as in later years, driving determinedly his mobility scooter in the middle-of-the-road daring both motorists and pedestrians to attempt to overtake him. An air of melancholy descended upon the village as everyone realised that they had witnessed the passing of an era.

Joe Fuller's subsequent funeral was a predictably grandiose affair with a large black hearse drawn by four horses which proceeded solemnly from the Manse through the village to the church. The cortege consisted of his numerous relatives – including four nephews, two nieces and their families, his siblings having passed away several years before – the presidents of the Rotary club, Lions Club and local charities and the mayors and mayoresses of Bedford and Luton. Altogether there must have been around four hundred people not all of whom could squeeze into the small church. Everyone agreed, however, that the service was beautiful and an appropriate send-off for dear old Joe. Even the sun shone appropriately as Joe was laid to rest in the church cemetery beside his wife.

Several weeks passed and the village resumed its usual and rather placid pace of life. Many wondered what would happen to the Manse and the lands around the village. It was, therefore with considerable interest that the village learned through social media that arrangements had been made for the will to be read in the village clubhouse one Sunday afternoon in May some six months after Joe had passed away. Conversations in the Six Bells inevitably turned to questions of who might inherit from Joe's will.

The day came for the reading of the will and, despite a chilly and persistent rain, the village turned out under their umbrellas to watch a procession of cars arrive at the clubhouse. This was an event worthy of Joe's importance for the life of the village and, although everyone knew that only the relatives would be privy to the contents of the will, they wanted to be part of the process.

Once the relatives had taken their seats in the clubhouse, the main doors were closed and the solicitor for Joe's estate took his place at a small desk in front of the assembled company. He opened a large folder, put his glasses on and took some time looking at his audience. There was Joe's oldest nephew Simon – a portly, ruddy faced, and well-to-do sixty-year old businessman, and his sallow faced wife Elizabeth. Seated next to them were the younger nephews John, Bert, Alex, and Cyril all of whom were some fifty years old. The first two had brought their wives with them. John had been married to Janet for thirty years. For some unaccountable reason she had brought her knitting with her and had obviously planned for a long will reading session. Bert's wife Alexandra, a blonde with long eyelashes and even longer legs, sat rather grumpily next to Simon and proceeded to spend some time observing her nails. Alex and Cyril, whose wives had been left at home either deliberately or by omission, had originally been identical twins but now one was decidedly fat, and one was thin. They sat in the second row behind Simon and Elizabeth and looked bored. After all, what else could be expected other than that good old uncle Joe would distribute his largesse to his relatives.

The solicitor, Mr Bentley, was an old hand at will readings which were usually conducted in his offices. In this particular case, however, the client's instructions had been clear that the reading had to take place in the clubhouse in Fulmersham and he would follow those instructions to the letter.

"Good morning, everyone and thank you for coming here today. My name is Richard Bentley and I have been appointed by my client, the sadly deceased Joe Aloysius Conrad Fuller, to conduct the reading of his last will and testament. I shall ask you to remain silent during this reading, but I'm prepared to address any appropriate questions for clarification at the end." He paused dramatically and looked out of the expectant audience.

"I, Joe Aloysius Conrad Fuller, being of sound mind do hereby write this as my last will and testament. To my dear nephew Simon..." Simon smiled. At last the old codger would recognise all the little things he had done for him during the later years of his life. "I bequeath the antique Victorian razor which my father used." The silly old sod had a sense of humour, thought Simon.

"To my dear nephews John and Bert, I bequeath the four paintings which I bought in a second-hand market in Vietnam and which have always been dear to my heart. I leave it to them to choose two each." John and Bert looked at each other in total bemusement. What on earth would they do with these badly painted scenes of Vietnamese life! Uncle Joe was obviously toying with their expectations.

Mr Bentley paused once more and savoured the rising tension in the room. "To my dear nephews Alex and Cyril, I bequeath my collection of second-hand silver plate and leave it to them to divide the collection equitably." Fat Alex looked at thin Cyril and wondered how much he could get for his share at the local car boot sale.

"To my dear great nieces and great nephews, I bequeath one thousand pounds to each." Well, at least we are now getting to the real cash and assets, thought Simon. "To my dear friends, the residents of Fulmersham, I bequeath a sum of one million pounds to be held in trust for the upkeep and improvement of the village." As one the nephews grunted in surprise and looked at one another. Each one was, however, confident now that their bequest would be substantial.

Mr Bentley continued. "The remaining estate consisting of my shares in various companies, the property of the Manse in Fulmersham, two hundred acres of farmland in Bedfordshire, the several properties in Bedford and Luton, the villas in the Dordogne, France and Tuscany, Italy and cash in all my bank accounts amounting to a total of twenty-five million pounds, I hereby bequeath to..." Mr Bentley paused again. God, I'm going to be so rich, thought Simon as he smiled expectantly. His wife Elizabeth managed to move her lips up in a grotesque sneer of satisfaction. John and Bert looked at each other wondering who would draw the winning ticket. Janet put her knitting down and Alexandra stopped looking at her nails. Each pondered the prospect of great wealth and how easy it would be to get rid of their husbands. Alex and Cyril both began to make plans. For all of them the future suddenly looked brighter and for a moment they failed to follow Mr Bentley as he went on.

"The remaining estate... I hereby bequeath to my beloved Natalia Adalina Borkov from Bulgaria whom I met online and who has been such a delightful source of support and consolation in my old age."

Mr Bentley had to pause while pandemonium broke out in the hall. Uttering a torrent of expletives Simon exploded in fury, his face suffusing to a beetroot colour. He swore would take the solicitor to court and seek to declare the will null and void. His wife Elizabeth hissed like a demented snake. John and Bert began exchanging blows, each blaming the other for not being kind enough to dear old uncle Joe. Janet threw her knitting down in disgust while Alexandra lit a cigarette in contempt of the no smoking signs.

Mr Bentley sighed and waited for the commotion to die down. "Ladies and gentlemen. I realise that the content of Mr Fuller's last will and testament might have come as somewhat of a surprise and each of you is, of course, able to contest its provisions if you so wish. Be aware, however, that it will be for you and your solicitors to fully justify such a contest. May I finish with the last words of Mr Fuller's will and testament which read – my love to you all and God bless the Internet!"

DREAMTIME
Alan Mackenzie

Tobias Goodfellowe felt so tired. It was not the tiredness as a result of any strenuous exercise nor from lack of sleep. It was just an all-pervasive ennui which seemed to affect every muscle in his body. Getting out of bed in the morning, getting dressed to go to work, making a cup of tea or even blinking an eyelid – every single physical movement had become an effort. He had first noticed the symptoms shortly after Christmas and had attributed them at first to an overindulgence in good food and wine during the season's festivities. So, he had begun to take more exercise, he went to the gym twice a week and drank much more water than was good for his bladder. But the symptoms persisted and, if anything, seemed to get worse. He went to bed early and could hardly get up the next day. He would fall asleep over the breakfast table and on the 7.46 train into London where he worked. He would nod off during coffee breaks and close his eyes during meetings. After a month his wife, Eleanor, began to show concern.

"Really, Toby, you must go and see a doctor. It's just not normal for a man of your age to feel so tired all the time."

"It's nothing, Ellie". Toby spoke through a yawn. "I've just been overdoing it at work." Eleanor looked at her husband sceptically. From her perspective overwork seemed the least likely cause of the problem. At the age of 41 Toby had a comfortable job in an insurance firm in a middle management position which placed no excessive demands on his energy. He had never shown any ambition to be a corporate go-getter and preferred the stability of a 9-to-5 job with all evenings and weekends free. Eleanor sometimes worried about his lack of ambition but, on the other hand, she counted the blessings of her uneventful life in her nice, semi-detached house in the suburbs. Whilst she occasionally regretted that they had had no children, she had ample time to devote to her rose bushes.

"Nevertheless, Toby. I shall book you in to see Doctor Mukherjee this Saturday. I'm sure he'll be able to give you some pills or something. Now, you'd better get off to work or you'll be late." Toby was too tired to demur.

On the train he scanned the Times and sighed at the bleakness of the headlines – air pollution at critical levels in London, New York and Beijing; leaders fail to agree on climate change accord; Thames blocked by giant plastic bergs; oil to run out in 20 years; nuclear power plant explosion in India; world population reaches eight billion;

uncontrolled wildfires in Australia; homo sapiens on the brink of self-generated extinction. Another normal day, he thought, as he sighed and fell asleep again.

Eleanor duly took Toby to the surgery the following Saturday to see Doctor Mukherjee where he related his symptoms.

After a somewhat cursory examination and monitoring of Toby's weight, blood pressure and heart the portly Doctor Mukherjee sat back in his ample armchair. "Well, Mr Goodfellowe, I can't see anything particularly wrong with your vital signs. We all suffer from tiredness from time to time, of course."

Toby stifled a yawn. "I've been looking the symptoms up on the Internet and I wonder whether I might be suffering from trypanosomiasis?"

Doctor Mukherjee smiled in an avuncular but decidedly condescending manner. "Very good, Mr Goodfellowe. You mean sleeping sickness? I must say I doubt that very much. You see, I don't think there are any tsetse flies in Rochester and, unless you have recently been in Africa or South America, the likelihood of sleeping sickness is very remote. Very remote, indeed". He tut-tutted and shook his head with a smile. "No, I think it is more likely to be some form of hormonal imbalance or lack of vitamins. What you need is something to give you a little more oomph, if you know what I mean." He smiled again as though he were enjoying a secret joke. He wrote out a prescription and ushered Toby out of his surgery with a cheery "I'm sure these will do the trick."

For the next two weeks Toby dutifully took his medication – purple and white pills of incomprehensible content swallowed down with water three times a day just before meals. They had no effect. If anything, the symptoms were worse. He was now sleeping eleven hours a night and was in a perpetual state of drowsiness throughout the day. Eleanor was now seriously worried about him and management and colleagues at work began to look at each other quizzically as Toby snored over his desk. It was about this time that the dream began.

It was a Monday night when he had gone to bed at 8 o'clock and fell quickly into a deep slumber. He was not normally conscious of ever dreaming but this time was different. In his dream he woke up in a strange fourposter bed with immaculate white linen sheets. He was alone and it was eerily quiet. He looked around the large dark wood panelled bedroom and saw the sunlight streaming through a bay window. He propped himself up against the pillow and rubbed his eyes. He no longer felt tired and, in contrast to most dreams, he had the most vivid sensations of light, smell and touch. It was as though he were actually awake. He slipped out of bed and walked to the window. The house was evidently on a hill since he could see a wide panorama of forests and valleys. To the left he could see rows of houses and what appeared to be factory chimneys belching out steam.

Just then there was a knock on the door. He jumped back into bed and said, "Come in".

"Good morning, Mr Goodfellowe. I trust you slept well?"

The lady entering the bedroom with a breakfast tray was smartly dressed in what appeared to be a blue uniform. She was an attractive brunette in her forties with an engaging smile that seemed to light up the room.

"My name is Anna and I am married to Andrew who will be up soon to explain why you're here. I'm sure you'll have lots of questions." She set the breakfast tray in front of him on the bed and stood back smiling. "Orange juice, tea, toast and marmalade! I hope you enjoy it. I expect you'll be wondering whether this is still a dream or not. Well, it is and yet it isn't. I'll leave the rest to Andrew." With that she smiled and left the bedroom.

Toby ate his breakfast slowly. He did not feel tired but was clearly asleep. This must be a dream, but every sensation was so vivid. The tastes of the tea, toast and marmalade were so real. As he set aside his breakfast tray there was another knock at the door and a tall, thin man stooped to enter the bedroom.

"Toby! It's been a long time." He gave a broad smile and with a shock of recognition Toby realised that this was the Andy Goldfarb he was once best friends with at college over twenty years before.

"My God, Andy. Is it really you? I thought you had disappeared off the face of the planet."

"In a way I did." Andy smiled enigmatically and sat on the side of the bed. "There's a lot to explain but it is so good to see you again." Suddenly Toby felt himself being shaken and the picture of the room and Andrew Goldfarb disappeared.

"Toby! Wake up, for goodness sake! It's past 9 o'clock and you'll be late for work. I honestly don't know what we're going to do with you." Ellie fussed around the bedroom as Toby, still almost comatose, got himself dressed.

"I had the strangest dream. You'd never believe it. I thought I met Andy Goldfarb again. You remember – I was a college with him."

But Ellie was not listening and pushed Toby unceremoniously out of the house. He got a late train into work and spent most of the day, yet again, dozing fitfully. When he got back, he went to bed early not only because he felt tired because he wanted to regain the dream, to find out what it all meant.

He fell asleep almost instantaneously and found himself again in the fourposter bed in the dark wood panelled room. The morning sun still streamed through the open bay window and he could hear birds singing in the trees below. There was again a knock on the door and Andy came in.

"I'm sorry we were so rudely interrupted." He laughed and shrugged his shoulders as he sat down on the bed. "This situation is never easy."

"I'm not sure I understand what this situation is. I'm in a dream and you're a figment of my imagination, I suppose?"

"You might think that and for my part you might be considered a figment of mine but I can assure you that I myself am not dreaming and I feel as real and tangible as this bed, this room, this house and the world I see outside."

"I definitely don't understand. But then it doesn't really matter because I'm dreaming, and I will wake up soon."

Andy smiled again. "Yes, you think you are dreaming, and you think you will wake up soon and return to what you think is your real world. But you have a choice, you know." Andy raised his eyebrows and inclined his head in an unspoken question. "But I'm getting ahead of myself. Why don't we go for a walk?"

Toby got up and dressed and followed Andy down the stairs to the front door of the house. Andy called out to Anna that they were going for a walk and they proceeded down a small flight of stone steps which bisected a neatly mown front lawn and ended at a latch gate in a tall hedge which gave way to what appeared to be a main road. They stood for a moment on the pavement and admired the scene in front of them.

To the left he could see the houses he had espied from the bay window of his bedroom stretching away into the distance and the factory chimneys with their columns of white billowing steam. From here he made out the familiar shape of Rochester Cathedral. To the right he could see nothing but trees – a sprawling forest which seemed to extend to the very horizon. The sky was a pale acrylic blue and he could clearly hear the birdsong. With a start he suddenly realised where he was. This was his hometown. This was where he lived. And yet it was not as he knew it. There were no cars on the road, no noise of trains, no bustling commuters, or blaring horns. And above all the air smelled sweet with none of the taints of oil, dirt or sweat that he was used to and for once he could hear the birds singing and the wind rustling in the trees.

"It's a pleasant town, isn't it? Shall we walk to the village green?" Andy set off at a brisk pace to the right with Toby following. As they approached a T-junction a small car passed them, and Toby realised that this was the first he had seen. Not only that - it was completely silent.

"Electric cars are amazing, aren't they? The combustion engine was outlawed in the West about fifty years ago now. They are still in use in some parts of the third world but even there they are giving way to electric engines." With that Andy strode off to the left towards an immaculately kept green surrounded by a circular row of shops and an oak tree as its centrepiece. Some children were kicking a ball around and screaming with delight.

Toby's confusion only grew as they stood before the old Victorian public house on the green. It was the Horse and Groom. It was his local pub. And yet somehow it wasn't. He kept telling himself that this was a dream and he would soon wake up.

"Shall we have a drink and I shall attempt to explain why you're here?" Assuming Toby's agreement Andy entered the pub and having ordered two pints of local ale, they sat down at a table in the snug. Apart from a young couple at the bar and the bartender himself the pub was deserted.

Andy sipped his pint and looked at Toby. "I know it must seem confusing. It was to me at first." He paused and then adopted a somewhat professorial air as though he were tutoring a new undergraduate. "I assume you know about the theory of a multidimensional universe?" Toby grunted an unconvincing assent. After all, there was nothing to lose since this was just a dream. "It took an exceptionally long time to prove the reality of this theory and even longer to put into effect the transition of an individual from one dimension to another. How to do this is even now known only to a small group of physicists and engineers, of which I have the honour to be one. But I can assure you that I am as real as you are and that you, here, are as real now as you are in the dimension from which you have come."

Toby laughed. It was, of course, preposterous but he was enjoying the dream and, for the first time in many months, he felt strangely alive and not at all tired. Andy went on. "In this dimension, which is one of an infinite possible number of dimensions, you still live in Rochester and you are still married to Ellie. But the world is quite different. Although the First World War still took place, man had the luck and ingenuity to develop hydrogen fusion as a source of power rather than nuclear fission as a means to wage war. What are known as fusion factories spread rapidly throughout the West and provided a limitless source of power with minimal pollution. Those are the factories you saw from the hill. The enormous wealth which was produced by this revolution in the production of power allowed the allies to support Germany after the war and undermine fascism. Hitler failed to become Chancellor in the nineteen thirties and died from a drug overdose in 1939. The Second World War never occurred, and the world has been relatively peaceful for the past hundred years. In the 1960s there were also rapid improvements in electric cars which finally allowed the prohibition of the combustion engine in the West and an enormous reduction in pollution." He paused his tutorial, sipped his beer and looked Toby in the eye. "This is a better place than the world you live in."

Toby tried to take it all in. "But why am I here? Of course, I know this is just a dream and that in a moment I shall wake up to the sound of the alarm clock and go to work as normal."

"It is not a dream and you are here because you have been chosen. In fact, I chose you as one of my best friends at college. You are one of the fortunate few who have the opportunity to change dimensions, to live in a world free of pollution, wars, poverty, overpopulation, and sickness. You're also free to say no. In which case you will remain in your universe and wake up as usual and will remember nothing of this experience. Over the next few weeks your tiredness will dissipate, and you will resume a normal life – whatever that means. I should point out though that, should you agree, this is a one-way ticket. Once you transition there is no way back."

On the way back to Andy's house Toby thought long and hard. It seemed he had little to lose and much to gain however ridiculous the proposition appeared. And he kept telling himself that this was just a dream so why would he not take the chance.

"There are just a few procedures to follow to effect the transition. We will put you to sleep and when you wake up you will be in your house with Ellie but in this dimension. Your tiredness will have gone, and you will remember nothing of this dream. You won't even remember having seen me again. But you have made the right choice, my friend." Andy smiled as Anna came back into the bedroom to administer an injection. The last words Toby uttered as he drifted off into sleep were a whispered thank you.

The next morning you will have to picture two dimensions or, rather, two films running in parallel. In the first, Ellie comes into a bedroom and tries to wake Toby who appears to be in a deep sleep. Then suddenly she realises he is not breathing. She screams and runs to phone the ambulance. The paramedics take their time to arrive but when they do it is clear that Toby is dead.

"I'm so sorry, Mrs Goodfellowe" says the kindly paramedic after trying CPR for more than 10 minutes. "It will be for the doctor to certify the cause of death, but it would appear it was a heart attack."

As Ellie tries to stifle her sobs, we can see the second film running. Here Ellie comes into the bedroom and shakes Toby awake.

"What time is it? I've just had the most amazing dream."

"Well, you'd better be amazingly quick to catch your train!" Ellie laughs as she musses his hair playfully.

Toby now enjoys his life. He now walks briskly to the station every morning breathing the sweet air and listening to the birds' chorus. He scans the Times on the train and reads about the new hydrogen hyperloop to France, the eradication of diseases in Africa, world population stabilised at three billion. He feels vibrant and energetic. His colleagues at work, of course, notice no change because he has always been that way. He has always lived life to the full.

On his forty fifth birthday Toby receives a letter from the Department of Population Control. He is expecting it, so it comes as no surprise.

"Dear Mr Goodfellowe, we are writing to inform you in advance of the statutory cull which will take place on your fiftieth birthday. You have, therefore, five years in which to make all necessary arrangements for your family and affairs before your life is terminated."

And in the back of his mind, lodged in some random neural synapse of his memory, Toby recalls his friend Andy's comment once that there is no such thing as a free lunch.

PARROT SKETCH
Alan Mackenzie

Killing his wife was not on John's shopping list that fateful Saturday morning. If it had been, he might have put it between the jam and lemons since he was of a methodical disposition. On the other hand, the act might have been intentional and, as such, would have been neatly noted as murder or manslaughter and followed the lemons on the list. But, as he looked in shock at his wife Amy's ample body lying like a sack of baking potatoes on the living room floor with the back of her head impaled on one of the points of the brass fire fender and at the gentle drip of blood onto the fireplace, he kept saying to himself that it was simply an accident.

He knew from the start that she was dead from the look of surprise in her eyes and the fact that she was not talking. While John had always been quiet, reflective, taciturn even, Amy spent every waking hour of her life in perpetual and usually one-sided discourse – talking to herself, to the radio, to the television, to her sister on the phone in Huddersfield or to the vast collection of knickknacks around the house. Animate or inanimate, nothing could escape Amy's stream of consciousness conversation. Now she was silent as if the volume had been turned off with a simple click of a button.

John sat on the sofa and wondered what to do. He had not meant to push her. He had just wanted her to stop talking so that he could explain why he was leaving her. Although you could never have said that the marriage was rocky - there had never been enough time for conversations to develop into arguments – they had both known for some time that it was at least shaky on the shingle. They had radically different outlooks on life.

John worked as the manager of a large supply depot on the outskirts of town. He enjoyed the order, simplicity and precision of the supply process and, above all, the feeling of space and quiet in the vast warehouse where the only sound was the low whirr of electric motors as the robots delivered and collected their pallets.

Amy, who could not have children, had decided early in the marriage that she would not work – John had a good job and earned enough to keep them both comfortably. She had instead devoted herself instead to the art of collecting. She spent her week trawling through the numerous charity shops in the town purchasing every conceivable type of knick-knack, gewgaw, bauble, curio, memento and objet d'art she could find. There were badly painted miniature gnomes which grinned lasciviously, cheap porcelain figurines, John Bull tankards made in China, souvenirs from holiday destinations she had never been to, vases of every different shape and type, bookends, ceramic frogs from Mexico, Easter bunnies and Santa Clauses. These she put on display in a growing collection of bookcases which filled every room in the house. Lately, having presumably exhausted supplies from the charity shops, she had progressed to larger items purchased from boot fairs and second-hand shops – old tape recorders and radios, ancient Singer sewing machines, a small piano and harmonium and even an enormous freezer which a delivery man had sweated to get inside the garage. This, she explained to John quite seriously, would come in handy in a nuclear war.

John got used to listening patiently as Amy explained her weekly purchases and how much of a bargain they had always been. Gradually, however, his heart sank when he came home and entered the house which seemed to quiver with the weight of her collections. The final straw had come as he stood on the doorstep after work one evening and she had announced that she had purchased an African grey parrot which she had installed in a cage in the corner of the living room.

"What on earth do you want a parrot for?" John had asked irritably.

"He's a lovely bird and ever so intelligent. I got him from Mr Bolger. You know, the pet shop on Dean Street. And he wasn't too expensive, and Mr Bolger threw in a cage without charge. I decided to call him Ronnie. Mr Bolger told me he'd be talking soon." After Amy, a loquacious parrot was the last thing John wanted.

As John sat on the sofa looking at the body of his dead wife and pondering what to do, he suddenly became aware of Ronnie in his cage in the corner. When Amy's headed hit the fender with a dull thud, Ronnie had squawked briefly but was now hanging upside down in his cage with his head turned and one eye with a pinprick pupil looking at him quizzically.

It was the parrot that had made him decide to leave his wife. That and the fact that he had recently met someone who did not collect anything and who actually listened to him when he spoke. Florence worked in the accounts department at the warehouse and come to his office one day to ask him about some misdirected supplies. From that first moment he knew he wanted to be with her and enjoy silences together.

Now, of course, his plan of leaving Amy with a peaceful, amicable separation and getting together with Florence was in tatters. He was sitting in his living room with the dead body of his wife in front of him. It was difficult to imagine how the police could conclude anything other than that this was an intentional murder or, at the very least, unintentional manslaughter. Either way he was looking at years in prison. He would lose his job, his pension, his house, not to mention his reputation. Above all he realised that he would lose Florence. He rehearsed in his mind how he would do the right thing and call the police and explain how this was just an "accident". But however he played out this scenario, however rationally he might be able to explain and however reasonable the police might be, he knew it would end badly. He looked up at Ronnie in the cage. Now sitting on its perch, the bird turned its head and fixed its black beady eyes on John. It was at this moment that he suddenly realised what he must do.

He stood up purposefully from the sofa and went into the kitchen to get a plastic shopping bag. This he put over Amy's lolling head taking care not to spill any blood on the carpet. He tied the plastic bag around her neck. He then returned to the kitchen for some bin bags. Given the bulk of Amy's body he decided it would have to be the 240 L size. He eased her feet into one of the bags which he pulled up to cover her rump and a second bag was put over her head to her waist. He then repeated the operation to make sure everything was covered and tied the body round with string. It was a makeshift body bag, but it would serve his purposes.

The body was too heavy to lift and so he dragged it into the kitchen, through the utility room and into the adjoining garage. He opened the freezer and removed the compartment drawers until there was just space for the body which he pushed in with some difficulty. He then set the freezer on maximum and closed the door. He then returned to the living room to find Amy's handbag and retrieve her mobile phone. This he used to book the next train to Huddersfield using her credit card. He then spent some time cleaning the spots of blood from the fireplace and the brass fender and hoovering the living room carpet. Fortunately, no blood had dripped onto the carpet itself.

John then went upstairs to their bedroom and packed a suitcase with Amy's clothes and toiletries. He retrieved her coat and handbag and put everything into her car. None of his neighbours appear to be out and about. He then drove to the train station car park. There he sent a text on her phone to her sister in Huddersfield saying that she would be arriving around midday for a surprise visit. He then put the phone and the car parking ticket into the handbag which he left in the car. He locked the car and just outside the car park dropped the keys into a drain. He then walked the five miles back to the house. This would be less conspicuous than taking a bus or taxi. Once back he phoned Amy's sister.

"Hello Vera. It's John here. Sorry to bother you but Amy asked me to give you a ring to say that she would be coming out to see you on a surprise visit. She said she'd be taking the 12.26 train. I think she said she'd be sending you a text."

"Why didn't she tell me earlier? You haven't had a bust up have you?"

"No, nothing like that. You know what Amy is like. Sometimes an idea just takes a fancy and she just goes with it."

"Well, as long as everything is all right."

John continued chatting for another ten minutes talking about his job and asking after Dennis, Vera's husband, who had recently had a heart bypass but was now apparently doing fine. He ended by asking Vera to confirm when Amy had arrived. It was now 10 o'clock on that Saturday morning. The train from Luton Parkway arrived at Huddersfield about 5 o'clock. He decided to wait until the evening to check in again on Vera. At all costs he had to keep up every semblance of normality.

He made herself a cup of tea and then reluctantly gave Ronnie some food. The bird looked at him with malicious distrust as he filled the dispenser inside the cage and even tried to bite him as he took his hand away. He then went out to the local shops pausing briefly to say hello to Jim his next-door neighbour who was now washing the car in the drive.

"What's Amy up to then?"

"Oh, she's just decided to go to Sheffield to visit her sister. She should be away for a week or so."

John was satisfied that the lie was breezily convincing. There was no panic, but he felt the heightened adrenalin of nervous tension. He was now a criminal covering his tracks and he had to make sure he got through the next few weeks.

Vera phoned at six o'clock to tell him that Amy had still not arrived.

"She probably decided to do the charity shops again and take a later train. I wouldn't worry. Let's leave it till seven and if she's still not there I'll send out the posse!" He kept it light-hearted, chuckling with exasperation at the unpredictability of his wife who was even now rigid with rigor mortis inside the freezer in the garage.

By eight o'clock it was evident to Vera that something was wrong. She had tried three times to phone her sister, but she was not answering. She insisted that John should contact the police.

He had never phoned 999 before and was unsure of procedures but by the time he got through to the police he had settled on the right tone of voice for an anxious husband looking for the whereabouts of his wife.

"I'm sure there's a perfectly innocent explanation, Sir. We get calls like this all the time and invariably the wife, husband, son or daughter turns up later surprised at all the fuss." The operator was calm and reassuring. There was nothing to worry about, but she would pass on all the details to the local police station which would contact him in due course. John phone Vera to tell her what had transpired. She was not at all mollified by his protestations that he had tried his best to get the police to go out and look for her.

"Bloody disgrace, that's what I say. All these taxes we pay, and they can't be bothered to go out and look for missing people!" John let her continue in the same vein bemoaning the general uselessness of most sectors of society until she got onto her general theme of the House of Lords and the Royal Family as parasites on the Commonwealth. Vera was still a paid-up member of the British Communist Party and regretted that Great Britain hadn't followed Lenin in 1917. John left it that if he had not heard anything by 11 o'clock that evening, he would get in touch with the local police.

About an hour after speaking to Vera John heard the police car draw up at the bottom of his drive and the reflection of the blue light flashing on the window.

"Good evening, Sir. Mr Elliott?" The two male constables were young, clean-shaven, and impeccably polite. John adopted a suitably haunted and anxious demeanour as he explained once again how his wife Amy had suddenly decided to go visit her sister. Sitting on the sofa on the other side of Ronnie the two constables went over the events of the day and seemed to take copious notes. John also gave them a recent photo of Amy.

"You say your wife took her own car and left it in the station car park?"

"Yes, she usually does this when she visits her sister. It's a long journey by car and it's easier by train. She is never sure when she might get back and, since I work irregular shifts, it's easier for her to leave it in the car park. This is not like her, you know, to just disappear." John choked back his emotion to add dramatic effect to his worry.

"Well, Mr Elliott. I think we've got all the details we need. We'll pass these on to Huddersfield and we'll check on the train station car park. You're understandably worried, Sir, but I can assure you that in most of the cases we deal with the so-called missing person turns up unharmed and unaware of all the concern she or he might have caused." As they went to the front door the first constable turned to John and asked casually "Just one last question and I'm sorry to have to ask it." He paused and left the thought hanging. "You haven't had any arguments recently with your wife? Would you say you are happily married?"

"We've been happily married for 15 years and, no, we never have arguments. Please do your best to find her."

Returning to the living room John caught Ronnie's eye. The bird was looking at him intently and he had the fleeting and fanciful thought that the bird knew what was going on. He thought about Amy in the freezer in the garage but that would have to wait. At least the police had not thought to search the house.

The next day the police rang to say that they had found Amy's car in the station car park. They had broken the lock and found inside her coat and handbag. They had conducted a search of the whole area around the car park and the station and of the route Amy would have taken with the car. They had launched a missing persons investigation and interviewed Vera in Huddersfield. John was asked to come into the police station later that day to give his fingerprints since were conducting a forensic examination of the car to see if there were any clues.

John took the next week off from work explaining to his understanding bosses the emotional trauma he was going through. The police were assiduous in interviewing his neighbours and came around several times to go through his story again. They explained, however, that with around 180,000 people going missing in the UK every year, resources were limited. A missing person notice with Amy's photo was, nevertheless, placed in shops around the town and there was even a mention of her disappearance on the local radio news bulletin. Jim and Alice from next door came round several times offering help and the occasional lunch since they were concerned that John would not be eating properly. His colleagues at work phoned him with moral support and he spent several hours on the phone with Vera who was convinced that Amy's disappearance had something to do with a capitalist conspiracy.

Several weeks passed and the phone calls and visits from police grew more infrequent. Vera phoned less often. John went back to work where his colleagues, and Florence in particular, were solicitous in their concern for his welfare. Gradually life took on a new, albeit Amy-less, normality. Except, of course, for the body in the freezer.

Once a month a police constable would pass by to keep him up to date on the state of the investigations. There were, of course, unfortunately no leads and the case of Amy Elliott's disappearance soon joined the other 150,000 cases of people who had apparently vanished in a puff of smoke. Not once did the police think about searching John's house for which he was grateful since he had no idea how to get rid of the body. While killing a person is always much more difficult than one would think, disposing of the evidence is an even greater challenge.

Six months passed and John's relationship with Florence blossomed into a true romance. He had at last found his true soulmate and he made plans to move in with her. He began to return progressively the vast collection of Amy's curios back to the charity shops and to sell off various items of furniture. A new and happy life beckoned.

Some seven months after Amy's disappearance John was in the living room one Saturday morning packing up yet another consignment for the local charity shops under the ever-watchful gaze of Ronnie when the doorbell rang. It was the police again – this time a there was an overweight middle-aged detective and a younger rookie constable. Yet again they sat on the sofa opposite Ronnie's cage.

"Moving out, are we, Sir?" The older detective's question sounded more arch than he intended.

"Oh, just taking some of Amy's things to the charity. She did love to collect." John tried to sound wistfully sad.

"We haven't given up, you know. We've widened the search to the whole of the UK and there's still hope of a lead coming up. I'm afraid though you must brace yourself for the fact that you may never find out what happened." The detective was brisk and business like but with a professional tone of understanding and sympathy.

Suddenly they were all aware of Ronnie stamping angrily on his perch in the cage and emitting shrill squawks. They turned to look at the parrot who was now fixing them with the piercing and almost malevolent black stare that only parrots are capable of. The squawks then gave way to a clearly intelligible human voice which sounded strangely just like Amy and continued to repeat the same instruction:

"Look in the freezer! Look in the freezer!"

The detective looked at the constable and then back at John whose face was now white as though all his blood had been drained.

"Noisy bird, isn't he?" The detective asked the question very slowly and then added meaningfully "Do you mind if we take a look at your freezer?"

WINDFALL
Richard Clifton

After a week confined to the cottage with 'flu, Brian was glad to be heading out on to the moors again. The small but barely affordable retirement home he and Rosemary had WAS nice enough but seemed claustrophobic after more than a few days. In addition, they had both found that their relationship was usually greatly enhanced by a certain amount of absence from the home, usually his.

He crossed the road, climbed over the stile in the dry-stone wall opposite their cottage and walking briskly, swiftly gained altitude. He was reasonably fit and wiry for a man approaching seventy but quickly got out of shape without regular exercise. He stopped for a breather after a few hundred yards and looked back. He could now see right over their mossy slate roof and spotted Rosemary working in the back garden. Brian loved gardens, but his involvement was strictly limited to sitting in them, admiring the work of others. Fortunately, his wife was never happier than when digging, planting, and weeding. At the moment it looked like the winter broad beans were going in.

After another half mile the cottage was out of sight. He was climbing a dome-like hill which was usually used for sheep grazing but was empty today. This side of the hill was fairly featureless, but he soon came in sight of the rocky outcrop near the summit. He started to regret the heavy sweater Rosemary had forced him to wear under his anorak against the wind and the November chill.

He made his way through the rocks and headed for the summit. On arrival he picked up a tennis ball-sized stone and added it to the little cairn at the top. This was not an official monument and all the stones were his. There were about forty all together marking the starting point for his many walks around the area.

Brian permitted himself the luxury of a morbid thought. These were not allowed at home. He wondered how high the cairn would be when he departed for the great retirement home in the sky. Big enough for him to need a step ladder he hoped.

He was a little out of breath and had already decided against a long walk. He went a short distance down the far side to where another dry-stone wall bisected the hill. This was taller than most at head-height and provided an excellent windbreak. He settled himself on a broad, flat stone in the lea of the wall where he had sat many times before. He fancied the surface was starting to acquire a polish from the seat of his corduroys. A barely legible sign lying on the ground nearby said "DANGER". On a previous visit he had tried to re-attach it to the wall with a piece of old wire, but it had fallen down again. The danger in question was the disused quarry on the other side, where about a third of the hill had been removed many years ago.

When comfortable, he removed a slab from near the base of the wall. There was a tall cavity behind it from which he took a bottle of Famous Grouse, about half full. Years of marriage had taught him that a drinks cabinet a mile or so from home was a grand idea. He set it up mainly out of respect for his wife, who hated alcohol around the home except at Christmas. Besides, after a strenuous uphill walk, a chap deserved a drink.

Brian took a few sips and thought about his current problems. There were one or two dark clouds on his horizon. Well, grey anyway. The biggest of these was called The New Bathroom.

The bathroom was the most decrepit part of the cottage with two of the four walls looking like they were original that is, pre-1800s. The 1960s extractor fan failed to keep things dry and, two weeks before, daub had become detached from wattle and left a large hole in the wall. Baths were accompanied by loud cheeping from birds in the roof space above.

Brian first tried to argue that this was a charming feature entirely in keeping with their rural lifestyle. There was no reply from Rosemary for a day. After this it was made abundantly clear that no-one would be invited for Christmas until the bathroom was fixed. Brian promised to do something about it. He had been looking forward to a little gaiety and over-indulgence with old friends during the festive period.

He wondered what the "something" he promised to do might be, given that their joint account only held a couple of hundred pounds, and he was a worse DIY man than he was a gardener. The job would take him months. This was made worse by the likelihood that Rosemary thought there was much more money available. Money was entirely his responsibility and he was normally fairly good with it, but retirement had been so much more expensive than he imagined. His lump sum had dwindled to almost nothing and both their pensions tended to be used up a week before month end.

The wind had dropped and when the sun came out it made his refuge into a little suntrap, even in November. He put the bathroom issue out of his mind, took another sip of Grouse and dozed off.

Brian was awoken by the sound of a car not too far away, probably in the quarry. He had never heard one here before. He knew that a drop of about a hundred feet into the quarry began just the other side of the wall. He looked for a crack in the wall and found a narrow one near the top. He could have looked over but, for reasons he could not explain, did not want to show himself.

Through the crack he saw a car pulling into the quarry floor below. It was a smart new BMW in dark blue. It turned to face back to the quarry entrance and slowed to a stop, the engine died, and a man got out of the passenger seat. A large man, in the sense that he seemed almost as wide as he was high, his blocky build emphasized by an expensive-looking broad-shouldered over coat. He surveyed the surrounding scene slowly, including a long look up at Brian's location and along the top of the quarry.

Brian took his monocular from his pocket and got a good view of the man's face, which was a good match for the rest of him. He was no one Brian knew from around here. His face was wide, almost frog-like except for the pale skin and dark crew-cut hair. He beckoned to the driver and pointed to a stand of bare trees by the quarry entrance. Brian heard him say something but could not make out the words.

A contrasting figure emerged from the car. A gangling youth by the look of him but his face was mostly hidden under a hoodie. Frogman walked over to the trees, kicked away some dead leaves and pointed at a spot on the ground. Then he pulled open his coat, fiddled with his clothing and peed on the ground, shuffling sideways, and altering his aim as he did so.

Walking back to Hoodie and pointing to where he had relieved himself, the Frogman gave instructions which Brian heard partially.

"...and about two feet deep," he said.

Hoodie opened the boot with his key-fob remote and took out a spade and a shiny metallic case, the kind a photographer might use to carry valuable equipment. He went to the designated location, put down the case and started to dig, presumably following Frogman's ingenious marking technique. His boss returned to the car and lit up a cigarette. Clearly excavations were not part of his duties.

Brian had started to form the distinct impression that something illegal was afoot. He took great care to keep from showing himself but tried to follow what was happening. Frogman kept looking up at the lip of the quarry, but Brian was sure he was invisible.

Two of Frogman's cigarettes later, Hoodie had dug the hole, buried the case, and covered the disturbed earth with leaves.

"something... hide the spade in the trees," Brian heard Frogman call to Hoodie. "We'll need it...something"

Hoodie returned to the car. Frogman offered him a cigarette, lit another for himself and they both leaned against the open boot of the car, smoking, and chatting inaudibly.

The big man finished his smoke first, threw the butt away and turned to Hoodie. In what looked like an affectionate gesture, he reached up and flipped back the young man's hood to reveal a thin face and a shock of sandy hair. Smiling, Frogman made a quip, maybe it was something like: "You're not such a bad-looking lad without the hood."

Then Frogman pulled a pistol from his pocket and shot Hoodie twice in the head, from temple to temple. The youth did not fall immediately but began to slide and was caught by the big man, who pulled a plastic bag from the boot and deftly slipped it over Hoodie's head. It was a bright orange bag, probably from Sainsburys. Brian could not read the slogan on it, but it almost certainly said "Try Something New Today".

The Frogman tied the bag very tightly around Hoodie's neck with cord or maybe it was wire. If the bullets had not killed him the strangulation certainly would. The bag was already sagging with blood when the big man tipped him into the boot of the car. Brian wondered if Frogman knew that supermarket carrier bags were not air- or blood-tight, for safety reasons. There would still be forensic evidence in the car. The rest of his mind was racing but failing to come up with any ideas on what to do right now. Brian pulled his mobile phone from his pocket. There was no signal. After some time, the first step became obvious.

He took a big swig of Famous Grouse.

****

Brian visited the outside toilet for the third time that morning before setting out. He told himself that it was Rosemary's chicken curry from last night, which was causing the problem, but it did not really explain the fluttering sensation in the pit of his stomach, which would not go away.

The door, attached by one hinge, almost fell off as he left the ancient structure. As soon as the new bathroom was finished, he would demolish it but today it was serving its purpose.

The plasterers and plumbers had been hard at work upstairs for three days and the bathroom was already looking very good indeed. So much so that Rosemary was beginning to say, very pointedly, that it would show up the rest of the cottage. Those remarks, and the astronomical repair estimate he had just received for their car, were what had decided him on his current course of action.

He ascended the hill opposite the cottage as he had done many times before. Realising he might be out longer than usual he decided to call his wife and apologise in advance, but his phone was unaccountably missing from his anorak pocket. There was no going back for it now, so he pressed on.

After twenty minutes of brisk walking Brian was at the dry-stone wall overlooking the quarry, his heart thumping far more than usual. He put it down to loss of fitness, as he had not been on his regular walk for a week or so. For some reason he had not felt like it.

He looked through the same gap in the stones he had used before. The quarry was deserted. He visited his rustic drinks cabinet at the base of the wall, finishing the Famous Grouse in a couple of hearty swigs, before starting the descent.

In another twenty minutes Brian had arrived at the trees beside the quarry track. He paused to get his breath and think about what to do next.

Eventually he emerged onto the track and tuned uphill towards the quarry entrance. He affected a jaunty stride. Just another guy walking the hills on a bright winter's morning.

There were faint washed-out tyre tracks at the quarry entrance but there was no telling how old they were. It had rained heavily a couple of nights back, so they probably were made before then.

Brian found himself almost hoping that the Frogman had returned for his money and was long gone but realised he would have to find out one way or another. He pictured himself driving a shiny four by four, and not the second hand one he had previously coveted. He walked through the quarry entrance.

Thinking someone might be watching he feigned interest in the treetops over the burial site and took out his faithful monocular. Perhaps the Blue Rock Thrush had returned. Still gazing up, he walked to the very spot. At last allowing himself to look down, he felt a mixture of blessed relief and bitter disappointment. The ground had clearly been disturbed since the rain, moreover he could see the shovel in the trees and not where he had left it.

Was it even worth digging? Surely the money would not have been re-buried? Unless the Frogman was helping himself to it piecemeal, as Brian had hoped to do. He retrieved the shovel and drove it into the loosened soil. It was enough to tell him that the case was gone or buried deeper than before. The disappointment was much stronger than the relief now. He dug a little deeper to make sure, then told himself not to be so silly. His new car was now only a fading dream.

"Looking for something?" said an amiable voice. It was Frogman. His accent was local, but it sounded like he had been away for a long time. Brian almost fell backwards. The look on his face must have been all the big man needed to know, if indeed he needed anything. Brian was not only a treasure hunter who struck lucky, he was a witness.

"I think I found what you were looking for," said the Frogman. He was standing at the quarry entrance, wearing his long coat and a friendly smile. He looked like the kind of fellow you could enjoy a pint in the local hostelry, and he would probably buy every round. Brian flinched as the big man drew something from his pocket. It was Brian's mobile phone, or an identical model.

"Just found it lying on the ground near where you're standing," said Frogman. You wouldn't have had to dig for it or anything."

The Frogman took a step forward, holding out the phone. Brian took a step back.

"Sorry to creep up on you, old chap" said the big man. "I fancied a bit of a stroll and left my car down by the main road. Luckily, I was able to trace you using the phone. You'd be surprised how easy it is when you've got contacts". He beamed and tapped the side of his nose conspiratorially with a forefinger. "In fact, I just dropped by your place to return it. Your wife said I'd just missed you and then I spotted you heading over the hill. I thought maybe you'd end up back here looking for it."

"Nice little place you've got there," Frogman continued. "Upkeep a bit pricey though, I guess."

Brian said nothing.

"Funny thing but I've lost something too, and it's left me a bit short. I was wondering if you could help."

Brian decided it was best to come clean, but only marginally. Another option he considered was falling to his knees and begging forgiveness, but that would have precluded option three, which was running away.

"You can have it all back," he said.

"Of course, I can," said Frogman confidently. "But actually, that would be a pain since I gather a lot of it is sunk into your new bathroom." He winked and added: "I spoke to the guy in the van outside your place. Twenty grand, that's a bit rich for a little bathroom".

"I've still got half," said Brian. "And I could sell my car."

"I saw your car too", chuckled the big man, shaking his head. "And to be honest with you, it's not just about money...as I'm sure you realise. And why didn't you take all of it? There was another 200 grand in the case".

The running away option popped immediately to the top of Brian's list and he turned and did just that. Behind him he heard Frogman say, wearily "Oh, for Christ's sake."

He had spotted a narrow path heading uphill through the tumbled rocks around the edge of the quarry and made for it. It might lead anywhere or nowhere. Beginning the ascent, he was expecting a bullet in the back of head at any time. He felt a little more confident when he remembered something from his extensive reading of crime thrillers. The general view was that a handgun was worse than useless at ranges greater than twenty yards, barring a lucky shot. He had a reasonable chance so long as his pursuer did not have a sniper rifle under his coat.

The path levelled out briefly and he risked looking back to see where Frogman was. The big man was fifty yards behind and in no hurry. He had reached the start of the path and began to trudge uphill. Seeing Brian looking down, he gave a cheery wave. The effect was somewhat spoiled by the pistol he was now carrying in the other hand.

Brian heard his pursuer shout something ending in "...just need a little talk" before he turned and fled up the next slope, which was rougher and strewn with rocks. At the top he saw he would have a short but near-vertical climb to negotiate.

He carried on, no longer running, and finding it difficult to maintain even a brisk walk. His heart pounded alarmingly, and he was getting severe twinges in his knees. He had been prone to twists in his ankles and knees in recent years and prayed he would not suffer one now.

A calm part of his brain was assessing his chances as he started the final climb. He was reasonably fit and half Frogman's weight. The big man was half his age. There were plenty of embedded stones for foot and hand holds on the near-vertical section, so he could probably scramble up eventually just as Brian was doing. The outcome was too close to call.

He grabbed handfuls of turf at the top and pulled himself up. He was confronted by another section of the dry-stone wall guarding the quarry. Beyond was flat ground leading gently down. Looking back, he saw that his adversary had achieved the flat area halfway up and was taking a breather. His face was very red, and he did not look quite so cheerful anymore.

Brian stepped back from the edge out of sight. He leaned against the wall and assessed the situation once more. He did not fancy his chances if Frogman completed the climb. He would be a lot faster going downhill. Anyway, there was nowhere to run to except his cottage where Rosemary would be thinking about making lunch. He would rather not introduce her to his new playmate.

He peeked over the edge again. The big man had started the final climb and paused. "I wasn't going to shoot you, you silly prick," he panted. "I could have ...kidnapped your wife...or something."

Brian caught from his tone he might have changed his mind about showing leniency. Having his wife held hostage was not an attractive option either. So much explaining to do. Besides there was no real chance he would be spared. If the positions were reversed, he wondered if he would have done the same.

"Come and get me," he said. He turned and ran from the edge, but only as far as the wall. Not yet, he told himself.

When he began to hear Frogman's heavy breathing, Brian picked a large stone from the wall and went to the edge. Frogman was halfway up the steepest section. As Brian lifted the stone above his head, the big man fired. Neither the pop of the gun nor the sound of the bullet passing close to his ear sounded anything like he imagined. It was a fairly good shot in the circumstances. He hurled the stone down, but it fell short and bounced high over the frog-like head. Frogman suddenly realised his predicament and began to scramble faster. Perhaps he was not so bright after all.

Strangely calm, Brian returned to the wall and selected another stone. The one he liked the look of was wedged tight and he spent seconds prising it out of the wall. It was twice the size of the first.

Frogman looked up and saw the big stone coming just before it hit him full in the face. He toppled slowly back, executing a graceful backboard somersault on the way. He hit the ground, did a much less tidy backward roll, and landed in a motionless heap where the ground started to level out.

Brian took the long way down and ten minutes later was observing the Frogman from the cover of a bush. He waited another ten but observed no sign of motion.

He now had time to assess his feelings and told himself he would be sorry if his opponent were dead. If he still lived, Brian hoped he might make an almost full recovery, apart from severe amnesia perhaps. And a little dementia would not go amiss. He wished this fervently but not quite enough to call an ambulance.

He eventually approached what he was now certain was a corpse. The gun was nowhere to be seen. He had to get his phone from the dead man's pocket or someone else would track him down. A fly landed on the bloodied face as he stared at the corpse. Surprising how a dead body can attract insect life so soon. He bent and reached into the deep coat pocket and mercifully it was there. Brian's heart bounded as he realised that Frogman's car keys were there also.

By January no one had reported a body on the moor, although there was the mystery of the executive car burnt out found abandoned. Not too surprising as it was not visible from the track or the main road, and the quarry side of the hill was not popular with walkers. Brian had driven up to the quarry entrance a couple of times, passing quickly and turning back. There was no sign of police activity or anything else. There might have been crow activity over the foot of the cliff where Frogman probably still lay. The ascent of the rough track had been a piece of cake in his brand-new Mitsubishi four by four.

A BRIEF ENCOUNTER
Alan Mackenzie

He knew he had little time to make his escape. The change of guards in their light blue uniforms took place at 9 o'clock every evening. It was at the same time that the elderly woman who sat in the corner of his cell on suicide watch also left for a short period. He would be left alone for 10 minutes. Just enough time, he thought. He was strapped to his bed and linked to a machine which he knew was feeding him drugs intravenously in preparation for the next interrogation tomorrow morning. This time, however, there would be no such interrogation. He would be free and on his way with the woman he loved who was, at this very moment, waiting for him at the train station. They would make a new life together far away from this repressive regime.

He watched the clock on the wall of his cell. At precisely 9 o'clock the suicide watch keeper stood up and walked to the door of his cell and opened the door to greet the uniformed guard. They whispered together for a moment and then closed the cell door softly after them. He immediately untied the straps which fixed his arms to the bed and removed the intravenous drip. He dressed quickly using clothes he found in a cupboard by the side of his bed. He did not recognise them, but they seemed to fit, and he found a wallet in the jacket. He opened the window carefully and looked out. His cell was on the second floor and he could see in the twilight the gates to the prison complex about two hundred metres beyond the lawn. He eased himself out of the window onto a ledge on the wall from which he grabbed the drainpipe. He was surprised at how easy it seemed to climb down to the ground. There were no searchlights and no guards patrolling the grounds. He ran over the lawn in the fading light and crouched by the prison gates which were open and monitored by a small guardhouse manned by one man he could see through the window. He watched and waited until the man turned his back and then crept through the gates.

He found himself on a main road which he thought he recognised as leading to the centre of the town and to the train station. Traffic was busy but he heard no alarm bells, no whistles, no police sirens. They had obviously not yet discovered his escape. He began walking to the centre of the town then hailed a taxi.

She had said she would wait for him at 10 o'clock in the station café. He did not want to be late. They had not seen each other for forty years, not since that fateful morning when he had left her abruptly to make his own way in life. It was a decision he always bitterly regretted since he knew that she had always been and would always be his only true love. A few months ago, he had received an unexpected message from her on his phone and after numerous exchanges of texts they had arranged to meet. This time he would never leave her again.

The taxi pulled up in front of the station just before 10 o'clock. He stopped at the entrance of the station café. There were few customers – two couples chatting animatedly and one elderly gentleman nursing a cup of coffee. Then he saw her seated with a suitcase in the corner of the café. Despite the forty years she seemed to him to be unchanged. The same auburn hair, the same smile of recognition as she espied him in the doorway.

"I expected you to be late – you usually were." She laughed gently as he sat down at the table with her.

"Not this time. And not ever again." He smiled and took her hand. The skin was as soft as he remembered, the scent of her body just the same. "It's been a long time and yet no time at all."

"And are we going to stay together this time or is this going to be a replay of Brief Encounter?"

He kissed her hand and whispered "Anne, I love you."

"Then you'd better get your train ticket."

They stood up, he picked up her suitcase and they went to the ticket machine. Then, hand-in-hand they walked to the platform. Just before boarding the train she turned and kissed him. "I'm so happy not to be Celia Johnson! And, by the way, I love you too."

****

The senior nurse in her light blue uniform is making her morning rounds in advance of the consultant. She enters the patient's room and takes in the wife and daughter by his bedside and the blinking light on the monitor. She feels for the patient's non-existent pulse, notes the time on her watch and turns to the wife who is holding her husband's hand with tears in her eyes while the daughter attempts to console her with a hug.

"I'm so sorry for your loss, Mrs Patterson."

"He passed just a few minutes ago. I know it was to be expected but it's still a shock. Alzheimer's is such an awful disease."

"At least we were both here at the end, mummy, and it was peaceful. Look how happy and contented daddy seems." The daughter smiles in sadness and squeezes her mother's hand.

Dabbing her eyes with a handkerchief the mother turns to her daughter and asks "There's something I don't understand. He kept repeating the name Anne. Do you know who that could be?"

"I think it's the name of his first girlfriend who died a few years back. But you know how confused he was getting towards the end."

Just then the senior nurse notices something clutched in the patient's left hand. She prizes it open and retrieves a train ticket issued the evening before at St Pancras.

"Well, I wonder how that got there."

THE PARTY
Richard Clifton

I arrive early as usual, hoping to have a quiet word with the hostess before the rest of the group turn up. Claire takes time to welcome me, like one of the long-lost, despite the fact that things in the steamy kitchen are approaching full panic stations. I accept the large amontillado, which is nearest to her hand, guessing the rest has gone into the trifle. I do not normally drink much at the beginning of festivities, but there will be no need to drive home on this special night. The dining room has no seating today other than the chairs around a carefully laid table, so I choose a comfortable chesterfield in Claire's garden room and look out at the setting sun. The rich sweetness of the drink and the cooking smells makes late February seem like Christmas.

A commotion at the door heralds the arrival of a huge bear-like man. If you do not know Oscar, you probably will not let him into your house, and even then, you will have second thoughts. After some prolonged and wholly inappropriate kissing of our hostess, he starts on me. I am not into man-kissing at the best of times, but today Oscar is sporting a ferocious designer stubble which looks like it might remove skin. I struggle valiantly in his grasp and manage to get away with an unpleasant smacker on the top of my bald head. "Haven't seen you for ages, old boy," he roars. Oscar's late wife was reputedly hard of hearing and we guess he assumes everyone is similarly afflicted. "Speak up, mate," I say, cupping my hand behind my ear in the ritual response to whatever Oscar says first. The equally ritualised gale of laughter comes back at me, but you have to wonder if he gets the joke. Even to his face, Oscar is often likened to Brian Blessed by those who remember the legendary actor. "Who?", Oscar always responds, genuinely mystified on every occasion. "Should be a good night," Oscar continues. "Even the twins are coming."

"I thought they were going to be in New Zealand for this." "So did I," he says. "Came back a few days ago. Ken and Rita are staying out there, apparently." The "twins" are actually Margaret and Dave, a very similar-looking and very reserved couple married almost twenty years, who have never been observed apart. There is speculation in some quarters that they are physically conjoined, but I know this is an exaggeration. Last year's Galadriel Day party was at my place and I witnessed Margaret's growing unease when her husband was dragged away to join an unsavoury all-male conversation.

As if by magic the twins appear in the room, having tiptoed in as soundlessly as usual. They look as if they might make a break for the door as Oscar bears down on them but elect to face the music bravely. The doorbell rings repeatedly. I guess Claire is tied up with something and I go to let the next guest in. It is my ex-wife Mary, bearing what looks like a giant black forest gateau. "Out of my way," she says. "This is heavy. "Nice to see you too, darling." I reply. I follow her to the kitchen where she is apologising to Claire. "I'm so sorry," she says. "It's shop-bought. The one I was making just went totally wrong. I couldn't believe it." I see Claire's eyes become shiny with tears as the tragedy of the failed gateau is recounted. That remarkable woman is blessed, or cursed, with a surfeit of empathy. Although not the eldest, she is surrogate mother to us all. It is entirely fitting that she is the hostess tonight.

I hear other guests arriving and I grab another drink to avoid the rush. I chat with Margaret and Dave about their time in New Zealand, Oscar having deserted them in order to terrorise the new arrivals. It turns out they had planned to spend Galadriel day there with our other friends but decided to come home early. "There were so many tourists," Margaret explains almost inaudibly. "And everything was so wild and noisy. We changed hotel twice, but it was the same everywhere." Her normally pale left cheek, and her husband's, were pink from recent encounters with Oscar.

The room quickly fills with the remainder of the guests. I count twelve but I have forgotten myself as usual. Thirteen altogether, so only Ken and Rita are absent. I wonder if it is unusual for so many old friends to stay so close. I know the majority from university days or not long after, and some even from school. It seems that our bonds have strengthened even more since the craze for Galadriel day parties started seven years ago. Our parties in earlier years were quite wild, with arguments over little things which once almost descended into fisticuffs. Claire was always there to spread the necessary oil, however, just as she is now. She hates it when her chicks quarrel and in the last few years we have rarely fallen out seriously, maybe mirroring the relative calm which seems to have fallen over the rest of the normally troubled world.

Claire calls the group to order and ushers us into the dining room where the table is set with more wine than we could possibly drink in one night. We sit and amicably decide where all the elbows will go. There is not much room. Claire and Mary quickly distribute plates of starters. Claire takes her seat last and makes an announcement. "For those of us who are believers in, well...something, and for everyone else..." she says awkwardly, "I think we should say some form of grace." We wait for her to start but then she looks at me pointedly and says: "How about you say something Dick? You're the writer." She knows very well I am not religious, and

I should be very cross with her, but tonight I'm not. I am only a writer of software manuals but I manage to make up something thanking Claire (not the deity) for the wonderful food we are about to receive and being happy to be with good friends on a special night. People are nodding. Then, unfortunately, inspiration strikes, and I also say we should be happy that science has revealed much of the truth about the world around us. I include the astounding fact that every speck of life on our planet shares a common ancestor with every other speck, including the asparagus and Parma ham which is our starter. That does not go down quite so well. Not all scientific truths are palatable I suppose. My ex-wife looks at me with a mixture of amusement and disdain, as if I am a wayward child.

The rest of the dinner party goes with a swing, if the laughter and general hubbub is anything to go by. Claire tells hilarious, and rather affectionate, anecdotes about her boozing and philandering husband, dead ten years now but still a source of amusement. My next-door neighbour, Daphne, takes issue with my implication that the human race is descended from asparagus and I wax lyrical about Darwin's tree of life for far too long. She falls asleep. Friends who were previously weight-watching are seen to dive into the gateau as well as the trifle and the twins, almost teetotallers, are getting decidedly tipsy.

Amazingly Oscar is sitting between them telling jokes, doubtless very smutty. Margaret and Dave are the perfect straight men, looking genuinely shocked but laughing anyway. Time passes enjoyably but I notice Claire is looking at her watch frequently. Not time already, surely?

"Guys, it's just gone eleven," she says eventually. "Maybe we should go into the garden and see what's going on." Instinctively we start to stack plates and Claire bursts out with laughter. "No washing-up tonight, people. I mean it," she says. "That's the upside."

We troop outside. It is a clear night and it is immediately obvious that the quality of the light is not what we are used to. The moon is setting in the west and has been completely usurped by another heavenly body. It is Galadriel, who looks down on us from the zenith. She is not as beautiful as the time of her last visit, seven years ago. Then her silver-blue hair streamed across most of the night sky and someone named her after the elvish queen with magical hair. So much better than her official name of Willis-Wang 2021, which is never mentioned now. Head-on we can see her face is craggy and scarred from her recent journeys close to the sun and perhaps from the impacts of the nuclear weapons which have failed to shake her resolve.

"You can actually see it getting bigger," slurs Oscar. "They said it would really seem to rush towards us in the last few minutes. When is it due to happen?" "Oscar," I say. "It's been in the papers every day for years. How come you've forgotten?" Galadriel's first kiss will occur at 11:28pm precisely, and its epicentre will be very close to Slough high street, only five miles from where we stood. John Betjeman will get his wish a millisecond before most of those who remember his poetry cease to exist.

Claire holds up her tablet with a talking head on the screen. "I've got Ken on skype," she says. "They're on a boat off the coast of New Zealand apparently. They can see what we are seeing on their screens. "They hitched a ride to the antipodal point I guess," I say. "It's off South Island." Ken and Rita are the lucky ones in a sense, along with the many other Brits who have gone there. They will live all of forty-eight minutes longer than their friends at home. That is how long it will take for the ripple in the earth's crust to get there. I have made the right choice, I think, because there is a chance that Ken and Rita's demise will not be instantaneous. For starters, the sea will most likely disappear from beneath their boat. Then they will have a brief interval for reflection, sitting on the seabed before mile-high tsunamis rush towards them at many times the speed of sound from all points on the compass. A spectacular sight but I will pass, thanks. The thirteen of us join hands in a circle and look up. We did not rehearse this last year on Galadriel day minus one. It is spontaneous. Galadriel fills so much of the sky that up and down are losing their meaning. Looking up now is a lot like looking down at the alps from an aircraft, and those cometary alps are getting ever closer. We are now the meat in a sandwich of two landscapes. I see that Claire looks content, almost happy. Always a little susceptible to New Age ideas, perhaps she believes that the coming impact with its heat and energy will somehow transform our friendship into something eternal. Anyway, she is with her good friends, everyone is calm, and her chicks will not be falling out with each other, ever again.

ALGORITHM
Alan Mackenzie

The hurricane season began early that year. The charmingly named Rebecca began swirling to the south of the Everglades at the beginning of June and the heat pushed up inexorably through the state of Florida into the Carolinas. In Sumter, South Carolina, people sweltered in temperatures over 40°C at midday and the power stations almost groaned in the effort to keep the tens of thousands of air-conditioning systems working. People made the usual evacuation plans in anticipation of Rebecca's arrival but for some reason the hurricane refused to move inland and the heat pall over Sumpter showed no signs of abating but remained like some unwelcome guest at a barbecue party. Few people ventured outside unless they had to or sought refuge in the coolness of the shopping malls. Everyone knew that bad things happen when it is hot.

On 10 June it was John Delaney Amherst's 21st birthday. It was yet another hot day as he woke up in his bedroom in his father's sprawling colonial style mansion on the outskirts of Sumter. He was excited because this was the day when, in all senses of the word, he would achieve his majority. He dressed casually in sneakers and shorts and went down to the breakfast room where his father was already seated at the table with his mother.

Senator John Delaney Amherst IV was 60 years old, silver haired and of ample girth which he managed, nevertheless, to squeeze into his white linen suit and waistcoat. For almost 200 years the Amherst family had been rich landowners in South Carolina and he himself had served the good people of that state as their senator for over 20 years. He had never been the brightest star in the Republican firmament, but he had connections, was assiduous in attending senatorial and congressional dinners and was generally considered by the party as "a safe pair of hands".

"Well, son, this is a special day! Happy birthday!" He beamed at his only son as his mother gave him an extra-long hug. Sun-tanned, tall, and athletic they were aware that their son was not over endowed with intellectual capabilities, but he was, nevertheless, a worthy scion of the Amherst family.

"Before you have breakfast, son, I have something I want to show you." The Senator stood up and led his son to the front door. "Close your eyes" he said as he opened the door. Parked on the drive, in front of the mock Roman porticoes of the main house, sat the latest model of a Maserati Gran Turismo gleaming red in the heat of the South Carolina sun.

"This is your birthday present, my boy, from me and your mom to show how much we love you and how much we are proud of you. We know you have a great future before you."

"Gee, dad, that is so awesome. Thank you so much." After a perfunctory breakfast John spent the rest of the morning admiring his car, investigating all the specs, and anticipating the envious comments of his friends whom he was due to meet that evening.

At 7pm that evening John drove his new and prized possession to Pete's bar on the outskirts of Sumpter. As the Maserati glided effortlessly into the parking lot, he was aware of people looking at him and by the time he entered the bar to greet his friends he knew he was nothing less than a film star.

John spent an increasingly raucous evening consuming copious amounts of beer and whiskey. Like John, his friends Mark and Peter were both rich kids destined to join their father's firms and perpetuate the inequalities of wealth which had made the USA great. It was not that they were unaware of the divide between rich and poor but for them, and under pressure from their families, they had easily learned to accept that this was a status quo, an ineluctable destiny which was useless to deny.

At around 11 o'clock John decided that he would take his friends for a drive in the new car. It slid out of the parking lot and onto the main road leading out of Sumter. It was still warm outside with few people about. John knew he was way above the drink-driving limit, but he was suffused with the joy of his new car and the fact that he was now 21. The world was at his feet and there was nothing he could not accomplish. It was precisely 11:13 PM when he made the fateful decision to test his car's acceleration. There was no traffic around and it was a straight road into the dark woods as he pushed the engine's irritable growl into a surge of power. Suddenly, just as it reached 100 miles an hour, a dark mass hit the front of the engine with a bang and bounced off the windscreen and onto the road behind the car. John slammed on the brake and screeched to a halt a hundred yards further on.

"What the fuck was that?"

"Must have been a deer or some kind of animal," said Mark. All three boys, sobered by the collision, emerged gingerly from the car, and looked back up the road. John took a torch out of the glove compartment and walked a few steps behind the car and shone it in the direction of the heap that lay on the roadway. It took several seconds for John to register that it was a human body. The legs were twisted unnaturally, and the arms were splayed out either side of its head from which a black liquid seeped onto the tarmac.

"Jesus Christ, John. What the fuck do we do now?" Peter tried to disguise the fear in his voice. All three, on the brink of their college careers, were all facing prison terms or worse if they were caught. They looked at each other quietly as a silent conspiracy formed. Apart from the eternal concerto of cicadas in the balmy night heat there was no sound in the woods and the road was deserted.

"Let's go," John said suddenly. They clambered back into the car and drove home. None of them noticed the young boy who was hiding in the trees and who had seen everything.

The next day John explained to his father how they had hit a roebuck on the way back from Pete's bar. Apart from a large dent on the bonnet there was little damage to the car. He felt bad about lying but he could not face the enormity of the fact that he had just killed a man nor the terrible repercussions if he was convicted of murder.

John took to scanning the local newspapers and two days later the Sumter Item carried a short report on the third page – State Trooper Richfield discovered the body of a 39-year-old man lying on a road to the east of Sumter. He has been identified as Jesse Baldwin, the proprietor of Baldwin Motors, Sumter. He leaves a wife and a son of 14 years. Trooper Richfield commented "This is obviously a hit-and-run probably by an out-of-state vehicle. We continue our investigations but have no leads as yet." Despite pressure from Mrs Baldwin the next few months saw little progress in the case which after a time got lost in cold storage, forgotten amongst the myriad of other robberies, fatal shootings and other murders which, in any event, produced juicier reports for the media.

In the first few months following that terrible night in June John Amherst fought with his guilt and fear and once even went so far as to contemplate giving himself up. But gradually his remorse subsided like sediment on the seabed of his conscience. By the time he graduated from college he very rarely thought about the accident although he always kept a photo of the red Maserati.

After college he set up a small hedge fund company in New York with a considerable amount of help from his father who had to sell off a large portion of his land holdings to provide the initial capital. But he made money and by the time he was 35 he was rich enough to be able to afford a house in the upper east side of New York and a suite of offices in the Trump Tower. He had not, however, achieved all this on his own. During his first year in New York he had been lucky to find a friend and mentor in Peter Dowden.

Born the son of an impecunious garage owner in Alabama, Peter had early on shown an innate grasp of how to, in his words, "turn a deal". He began by selling cigarettes and alcohol in high school but soon found there was more money in marijuana. He was clever but undisciplined and had several brushes with the local sheriff for speeding in his dad's second-hand Porsches. Somehow or other he nevertheless managed to avoid any jail time. At the age of 18, however, he decided that the only way to make real money was to make his way to New York and to try his hand in Wall Street. He set up a small company which invested in Internet start-ups. The business did not, however, do well and was hard-hit by the fiscal crisis in 2008. It was at that time that he met John Amherst in a bar on 10th St, Manhattan and, together, they decided to establish Amherst Dowden Capital. With Peter's cunning and John's money they would go on to put their firm successfully on the financial map. After all, they were both southern boys. They also both believed in the essential goodness of the market and that the only bad capitalist was a dead one.

Together John and Peter were almost the perfect team. Peter was the intellectual engine of the firm – he could read the markets and devise strategies that would maximise financial return. He was also good at picking out people who could work in a team for the good of the firm. John, on the other hand, was the outward face of the firm. He had inherited his father's natural bonhomie and rather oleaginous smile, glad handing potential investors until they felt obliged to hand over their money.

All went well with Amherst Dowden Capital until that June day in 2021. It was a Friday after a bad week on the markets. Black Monday had been succeeded by black Tuesday and Wednesday until eventually the whole week seemed to have descended into a dark slough of despond. Shares had fallen by 25%, firms were declaring insolvency, profits were non-existent and even the Chinese seemed to be withdrawing their investments. Ripples of panic followed the financial markets from Shanghai through Hong Kong, Frankfurt, London, and New York while John fended off his shareholders and creditors with less and less credible assurances of good times to come. He was relieved to have some respite at the weekend.

On the Monday morning, however, the situation had not improved. Despite a rallying of markets across the globe the assets of Amherst Dowden Capital were in dire trouble. At 8 AM Peter rushed into John's office.

"Jesus Christ, John. We're fucked!"
John was hunched over his two computer screens which looked like monitors attached to patients on life-support. All the shares in which his company had invested were down by 40%.

"How bad is it?"

"I reckon in total we're about 20 million in the red."

John sat back in his executive chair and the two of them contemplated bankruptcy.

Then Peter looked at John and said slowly and deliberately "There is something we could try although it's a risk."

"Well, come on then, what is it and what is the risk? "

"I got this guy on the team."

"What do you mean, you got a guy?"

"He's a brilliant young graduate from MIT. Had a scholarship to Harvard too and came out summa cum laude and all that shit. He's got this computer algorithm for playing the markets which he reckons is infallible. I haven't wanted to take the risk until now but, hell, we've got nothing to lose. He'll want paying, of course."

John considered the idea briefly, "Okay. Let's do it. Give him part of the portfolio and tell him we want results in three days. What's this guy's name anyway?"

"Michael, Michael Baldwin. Likes to be called Mick."

Within three days Mick's algorithm had worked like magic on that part of the portfolio assigned to him. He was up ten million dollars. Peter and John together agreed to allow him to apply the algorithm to the whole portfolio. A week later the firm's shares had recouped all its losses. Two weeks later its value had increased by a healthy 20% and Mick had been given a generous bonus of two million dollars. John decided it was time he met this Wunderkind.

Mick entered John's spacious office with a quiet confidence. He was a tall, athletic young man with close-cropped hair and an almost iridescent ebony skin. John came from behind his desk to shake the young man's hand.

"Well, Mick, I'm real glad to meet you and thank you in person for the great work you've been doing. Take a seat."

Mick said nothing in return but sat down in one of the plush leather seats in front of John's desk. He looked around the office casually taking in the views of New York through the tenth story windows, the grand colonial style desk on which reposed John's computers and the bookcase behind which contained few books but numerous photos of the Amherst family and, in pride of place, a model of a red Maserati.

"Can you tell me how this algorithm works, Mick? In layman's terms, of course. Math was never my strong suit." John's tone was all brisk, executive efficiency with just a hint of humility.

"Like all algorithms it's based on a lot of data and a lot of probabilities which it recalculates in nanoseconds and then optimises the time at which shares or currencies are bought or sold. In some ways it's like a virus. It replicates but adapts to circumstances. But, as you know, markets are fickle so you can never be certain of anything. La donna e mobile!" Mick chuckled at the operatic allusion which went over John's head. "It's also got an added ingredient which shall forever remain a secret." He smiled as he tapped his nose with an elegant forefinger.

"Well, Mick, as long as the recipe produces profits for the company, I'm not sure I need to know what ingredients go into the cake mix. I just want you know how much we appreciate all your hard work." John stood up to indicate the interview was at an end. There was a pause which went on just a little too long as Mick looked into John's eyes but made no move to stand up.

"Mr Amherst, before I go there are a few things you need to know. First, as of this moment I quit. You have the algorithm and you paid me for it. I have no comeback on you and you have none on me. It may continue to make you profits. I sure hope it does, for your sake." He paused. "On the other hand, it may not."

As John sat down, he made to speak but Mick lifted his hand to show he hadn't finished. "The second thing you need to know is that you can't stop it. The algorithm, I mean. The moment you try and interfere with it, it will reverse engineer itself and it will buy and sell under the worst not the best conditions. Clever things, viruses."

"What the hell are you talking about?" John cast an eye of his two computer screens where he suddenly saw his share prices falling.

"Well, John. You don't mind me calling you John, do you, now that I'm no longer your employee?" Mick smiled almost triumphantly. "You see, we're both South Carolina boys from the same neck of the woods even. We both want money, houses, cars, family, even some degree of happiness, I guess. But there's one thing that separates you and me – I want justice."

"What the fuck do you mean? I think it's time you got out of my office." John's voice was rising in anger.

"I like Maseratis. I might even buy one now you've paid me." Mick's voice was soft and quiet as he nodded his head towards the model on John's bookshelf. "I remember seeing a red Maserati once. Must've been fourteen years ago on a road just outside Sumpter."

John's face blanched. Baldwin. That was the name. The name of the man he killed and whose body he left on the road on that hot night in June so many years ago. And the name of the man who sat before him.

"I watched you drive off that night and leave my daddy on the roadway like some piece of roadkill. My mom and I, we tried our best to get the police to investigate properly. I even remembered the licence plate. But you know how it is – the police weren't really interested or had too much to do and once that state trooper had implicated an out-of-state vehicle who the hell was going to believe a poor twelve-year-old black boy's recollections. Besides which who's going to finger the son of the senator?"

Mick stood up and walked to the door to address his last words to John slumped in his chair.

"By the way, John, the algorithm will still work through the programs on your remote servers even if you try and turn off all your computers here. I reckon most of your assets will be sold at a loss by the end of the week. You'll be bankrupt." He paused and took a long, pitying look at the heir to the Amherst dynasty.

"You gotta know, John, that I don't hate you. I know it was an accident. But you gotta understand that actions have consequences and that all lives matter."

TATIANA
Alan Mackenzie

Colin Watson was lonely. He was thirty-nine years old, still lived with his mum and dad in Wood Green, London and was still looking for the love of his life. It was not that he was unattractive to the opposite sex – he had a full head of black hair; he was not overweight and worked out twice a week in the local gym. He had a ready smile and was easy going with his mates at the bus company where he worked as a bus driver. He liked to think he was in the prime of his life – indeed, that was what his mum kept telling him:

"Colin, it's about time you settled down. You're a lovely boy and there's no end of girls out there who'd jump at the chance." For his mum, who had turned 65 and had been married to his dad for 45 years, the pool of "girls and boys" covered anyone between 20 and 60. "What about that Trish you were seeing? She seemed ever so nice."

He'd taken Trish out three times – to a local dance, to an arts cinema in North London to see a re-showing of Last Year at Marienbad which both had found impenetrable and finally for a curry along Green Lanes which had given them a gippy tummy for a week afterwards. But it was not the curry that had spoiled the potential romance nor coma inducing arthouse films. Colin's greatest problem was his shyness. Once any conversation had to go beyond the exchange of pleasantries or comments on the weather, he became tongue-tied and almost inarticulate. He could talk about the bus routes of North London, of course, but he knew that this was of little interest to other people. Consequently, most of his brief relationships ended after three or four dates in a sad silence, a brief peck on the cheek and an unfulfilled promise to give each other a call.

He had tried almost every avenue to combat his affliction. He had enrolled in evening classes to improve his social skills but his pottery making had been such a disaster after he had whisked a wobbly vase off the wheel and hit a fellow student that he had been asked by the teacher not to return. His attendance at the classes on the history of Byzantine art was no more successful since he invariably began snoring after half an hour of every lecture. He had even tried hypnotherapy but found that 70 quid an hour was a little steep just for a nap.

It was not until his friend Dave suggested dating sites that his life changed. He was not particularly interested in computers – he much preferred driving a bus but for his fortieth birthday he finally invested in a powerful laptop, installed Wi-Fi, and began surfing the world. It was a revelation. Dave proposed a whole list of dating apps and contact sites which he himself had used (not always appropriately) and Colin began to converse with people in such far-flung lands as Malaysia, Australia, Chile, Russia and the USA. He enrolled in Godatenow, Yourtravelmate, Letmedate and Dreamsingles and was amazed to realise how many people were reaching out for company and consolation. He suddenly found it easy to conduct conversations by text and some days even by video. He frequently spent three or four evenings a week contacting the world. For once in his life he felt both liberated and empowered. But his life was to change forever that evening when he logged in to GetMeHitched.com.

He had had yet another argument with his mum after work about being single and getting old and had decided he would finally do something about it. He was amused by the name of the site which sounded preposterously desperate but GetMeHitched.com promised to provide the woman (or man) of everyone's dreams from a cornucopia of international contacts. He paid his remarkably modest subscription, filled out the online form for his preferences – single, aged 30 to 40, slim, brunette, vivacious and with an interest in buses and uploaded his best photo. To his surprise the site came back within half an hour with ten proposals in priority order. There was Lisa from Melbourne, Tanya from Texas, Elizabeth from Ontario, and Ying Yue from Shanghai whose name he learned from Wikipedia meant reflection of the moon. But it was number five who captured his heart – Tatiana from Novosibirsk.

He had no idea where Novosibirsk was and had to look it up – a large industrial city in Russia with almost 2 million people located on the river Ob in Siberia and some 3300 miles away from Wood Green. Not that any of this information mattered much to Colin compared to the photo which Tatiana had posted. She had long, luscious brown hair, large brown eyes, high cheekbones, ruby red lips, and an engaging smile. The photo seemed to embody a sensuality and exoticism which quite overwhelmed Colin. From that moment on he was besotted.

Colin and Tatiana began by corresponding by text once or twice a week, but this soon became a daily assignation. The six-hour time difference made things a bit complicated, but Colin was able to overcome this by changing shifts at the bus company. Tatiana's English was rudimentary but soon improved while Colin began learning Russian. She told him she was a primary school teacher and lived with her parents. Her father worked in a large instrument factory where her mother was in charge of catering. She had a sister, Svetlana, who had married a successful engineer and lived in Moscow.

After a month of texting they had their first video call on zoom. Colin had shaved, showered, and put on aftershave for the occasion as though this was a real first date and he had dressed in a tie and jacket which he thought might reflect an appropriately casual insouciance. He had difficulty seeing her properly through the zoom connection, but Tatiana explained that the lighting was bad in her room in the communal flat in Novosibirsk. In any event he had a printout of her photo and could imagine her smiling and laughing. Despite the language difficulties their conversations gradually became more intimate and after three months Colin was convinced he had found the love of his life. He melted as she said, "I love you too." Those liquid L's and soft sibilants of the Russian language were like waves on a tranquil seashore. Finally, they agreed that Tatiana should come on holiday to Wood Green where they could meet in person and decide whether they had a future together. Colin agreed to send her the money for the train fares as the airfares were prohibitively expensive.

Tatiana told her parents of her intention to go on holiday to London to visit the man she had fallen in love with. They were overjoyed at the prospect of their second daughter finally leaving the nest and gave her a tearful farewell at Glavny train station one chilly October morning. It was a sixty-hour journey to Moscow and Tatiana was exhausted by the time she arrived to see her sister Svetlana waving on the platform. She stayed overnight at her sister's flat and in the morning took the train to Paris which took another thirty-seven hours. Finally, after over five days' travel she boarded the Eurostar in Paris for the short journey to London St Pancras.

Tatiana was due to arrive at 9:39 AM at the Eurostar terminal in St Pancras. Colin was both excited and full of trepidation. He got up early and dressed in a suit and tie. He wanted to make the best impression. He had not told his parents of Tatiana's visit. He wanted it to be the surprise of their lives. He bought some flowers at the local florist and took the tube down to King's Cross in plenty of time. At 9 o'clock he was already waiting impatiently at the Eurostar arrivals.

By 0945 the travellers from Eurostar were exiting into the concourse of St Pancras. Colin clutched the photo of Tatiana and scoured the crowds. After fifteen minutes he still could not see her. Suddenly he was confronted with a lady with short auburn hair in a large black overcoat trailing a suitcase.

"I Tatiana – you Colin?" It was obvious that she was Russian or at least Eastern European, but this was not the Tatiana in his photo. This was not the woman he had fallen in love with. Where was the long, luscious brown hair, the large brown eyes, the high cheekbones, the ruby red lips, and the engaging smile.

"I think there's been some mistake." Colin was flustered and suddenly afraid.

"No. No mistake. I Tatiana. You Colin. You invite me."

Tatiana smiled rather lopsidedly with thin lips to reveal the gold canine tooth on the right-hand side. Colin reacted with horror and backed away towards the exit of the station. Tatiana followed him protesting as he broke into a run and rushed out into St Pancras Rd. The number 46 bus passing by had no time to brake and hit him full on. His body passed under the wheels and people heard the strangulated cry as his rib cage was crushed and his left leg was broken. His friend Dave was driving and had no idea it was Colin until he stopped the bus 50 yards further on and walked back to see the body. He had clearly died instantly.

Tatiana stood in shock at the scene and then turned slowly back into the concourse. Perhaps it had been unfair to use Svetlana's photo but then her sister had always been more attractive than her. She went to the coffee shop, ordered a tea, and sat down to contemplate her next move. She took a pocketbook out of her handbag and flipped the pages. Her next appointment, one of six planned for the day courtesy of GetMeHitched.com, was in half an hour. Perhaps she would have better luck with John Thatcher from Dagenham.